THE CONQUERED

REBELS

BOOK ONE OF THREE

THE CONQUERED

Dafydd ab Hugh

POCKET BOOKS

New York   London   Toronto   Sydney   Tokyo   Singapore

POCKET BOOKS, a division of Simon & Schuster Inc. 1230 Avenue of the Americas, New York, NY 10020

A VIACOM COMPANY

This book is published by Pocket Books, a division of Simon & Schuster Inc., under exclusive license from Paramount Pictures.

ISBN: 0-671-01140-5

First Pocket Books printing February 1999

10 9 8 7 6 5 4 3 2 1

Printed in the U.S.A.

Historian's Note

The present-day sections of the Rebels trilogy take place during season four of *Star Trek: Deep Space Nine*.

THE CONQUERED

PRELUDE

THIRTY YEARS AGO

"MY LORD, what may I bring you from our Prophets?" Sister Winn asked, as Gul Ragat and his Cardassian friends and colleagues roared with laughter at her impishness.

"From your *Prophets?*" echoed another young Cardassian, a gul in the Cardassian land forces. The boy—*Akkat*, Sister Winn remembered—wore a sneer that he obviously practiced before a mirror. His voice held a nasal quality found to a lesser extent in most Cardassians—probably a species trait—but grating to Bajoran ears nevertheless.

"Yes, Lord Akkat," said the priestess, bowing low to the boy who was only a little more than half her age. "The Prophets offer peace and hope to all, even Cardassians."

The council room was dim and cool, with harsh dark-wood chairs surrounding a severe table. Communications equipment, viewers, touch pads adorned the place settings, along with a chalice of Kanar for each man.

There were four other Cardassian lords and overlords around the table, including Winn's own master, Gul Ragat. They all laughed at her last statement, and Gul Dukat, master of *Terok Nor* and one of the governors of Bajor Province, probably in line to succeed Legate Migar as prefect of all Bajor, nudged the young colonel. "Are you going to allow a Bajoran priestess to speak to you that way? Offering you leftover blessings from her gods— *after* the Bajorans take what they want?"

If Akkat was haughty before, he was positively livid now. He leapt to his feet, knocking over the heavy Cardassian-style chair. His facial ridges stood out stark and white . . . an ominous omen.

Sister Winn was used to such Cardassian outbursts, and she knew what she had to do. She had survived most of her adult life under Cardassian occupation, and she was no fool. Winn fell to her knees, bowing until her face was pressed against the floor. "Please, My Lord! I meant nothing by it. I spoke in error, and I beg your indulgence."

Akkat pushed his way around the table, teeth clenched; he even shoved Gul Ragat out of his way in his rage—a bad move, as the gul, though just as young, outranked him by quite a margin of social status. "Wretched beast! Get up off the floor and accept your correction like a—like a Cardassian child would!"

But the priestess's own master rose, now annoyed at Akkat for pushing him. "Akkat!" he shouted, deliberately ignoring the lesser soul's title (a serious insult in Cardassia). "Don't touch my servants! Take your hands away; if you want to damage property, damage your own! I still have use for mine."

Ignoring the warning, Akkat swung his open hand at Winn's face. She did not try to shield herself from the blow; she was too canny from years of experience. Instead, the priestess twisted her head in time with the blow to minimize impact, then allowed herself to fall in the same direction, exaggerating the force. *Then* she covered her face with her arm and again begged forbearance.

Gul Akkat looked uncertainly at his colleagues, aware he had just struck a woman—a Bajoran woman, to be sure, but even so. When Gul Dukat himself turned an angry gaze at the young gul and said, "A Cardassian does not lose his temper around Bajorans," Akkat slunk back to his seat, his face flushed with embarassment.

Still stretched out on the floor, Sister Winn felt several moments of triumph that she had finally goaded the weakest Cardassian into humiliating himself. She had subtly taunted him for several minutes: nothing overt enough to truly give him cause to strike her (in which case, the others would have ignored the incident), but sufficient needling that he lost control at the most innocuous of statements. Then Winn felt a twinge of her own conscience; she tried to tell herself that it was a "strategic" maneuver, trying to make the lords and overlords lose confidence in one of their own. But that was a lie: it was a petty, vindictive act and not in keeping with the teaching of the Prophets.

She rose to her knees, bowed again to Lord Akkat, and said, "I humbly beseech your pardon for the disrespect I have shown." But she was not talking to the young pup of a Cardassian; in Winn's heart, the words were directed skyward, to those who heard even the quietest heartfelt prayer.

The rest of the meeting proceeded routinely. There were no secrets discussed, and the lords took no precautions against any of the servants, including Sister Winn, listening in. The matters were run-of-the-mill administrative reports and the issuance of standing orders that were already available over the subspace newsmitters anyway. It was more a formal event, held so that four guls and the legate could set themselves aside as the administrative (and military) leaders of the subcontinent.

In fact, it was quite an honor that Gul Ragat was even allowed to attend, as he excitedly told Winn during a break, walking alone in Legate Migar's garden with only a "personal priestess" in attendance. "Winn, you have no idea how extraordinary it is for a mere provincial subgovernor to be invited to Legate Migar's for the monthly bulletin-tea!"

"I know it is a very great honor for your lord-ship," said the priestess.

"A great honor, indeed." The young gul turned serious for a moment. "I'm afraid it's *too* great an honor, Sister Winn."

"Oh, surely not, My Lord!"

"Relax, Winn. We're alone now." The boy turned an astute face to the priestess, who felt the most absurd impulse to comfort the lad. "I'm not disparaging my family; my lineage is if anything even grander than that of Legate Migar himself . . . and the old man knows it. But since when does the provincial subgovernor of Shakarri and Belshakar-ri rate an invitation to the bulletin-tea?"

Winn thought for a moment; the child had a point, not that she particularly cared much about Cardassian rules of protocol. "Perhaps they are grooming M'Lord for a promotion?"

Gul Ragat grinned and chuckled, shaking his head. "It's called a grant of honors, not a promo-tion! Silly girl. But I understood what you meant, and I confess that I've been thinking the same thought myself . . . and damning myself for being an ambitious man even for thinking it."

Sister Winn said nothing. The garden was too tight, too martial, as were most Cardassian arti-facts. The trees were planted too close together, like soldiers in ranks, and the paths were straight as Cardassian roads, intersecting with each other at precisely defined angles that one could see for many steps ahead. Sister Winn preferred either the soothingly planned garden of the Kai, which she had seen only once in person but had walked often in her dreams, or the rambling, meandering footpaths of the woods outside her native village.

Gul Ragat stopped and sat upon a stone bench, watching the Fountain of Discipline: the spigots fired in bursts like a weapon, launching a cylinder of water into the air, arching over the hexagonal plaza to land squarely in a small catch-basin on the other side. Sister Winn did not, of course, sit beside the gul; it would have surprised him and made him uncomfortable . . . though he would not have punished her for it.

He might also have taken the wrong idea. One night, he had somewhat drunkenly explored his options with Sister Winn, but she made it clear (by "failing to understand" his advances) that she may be his servant, but she was not his toy. She much preferred somewhat an air of formality, to ensure the two did not get too close; Sister Winn had no illusions about their relationship, the conquered to the victor.

"Winn, I'm . . ." The gul trailed off; Sister Winn did not prompt him—it wasn't her place, and she hoped he wouldn't decide to confide in her anyway. "Winn," he said again, "I'm afraid."

"Afraid, My Lord?"

"Afraid of the added responsibility. Afraid of what we're doing—" Gul Ragat froze in midsentence, looking around himself in an almost comical paranoia. "Sister Winn, do the Prophets truly exist?"

"I have spoken with them frequently, My Lord." Ragat did not ask whether they answered her when she spoke.

"Winn, I'm—*afraid* for the soul of Cardassia, what this occupation is doing to us. I know Akkat; we go way back."

He's going to tell me what a good person he is, thought the priestess with amusement.

"Winn, Akkat is such a good man! I know you feel hurt and humiliated by what he did, striking you like that for no reason. You're confused, and you're angry—furious at us! No, don't deny it; I know how you Bajorans feel about this occupation. And to tell the truth, I even understand it. There's no heavenly reason why Cardassians are any better or superior to you people. I understand you completely."

Sister Winn said nothing, not trusting her self-control. She decided it was politic to bow her head; she also put her sleeves together and savagely gripped one hand in the other to prevent them moving of their own accord where they wanted to go. *Oh, Prophets of Bajor, please forgive and take from me my violent impulses!*

"But it's this damned military thing," continued the young gul, little aware of the emotions he was stirring in the normally placid Sister Winn. "It warps us, makes us the sort who—who strike an

7

old woman because she reminds us of how uncomfortable we feel, trying to civilize the Bajorans by force . . . trying to force our civilization upon the Bajoran civilization, I should say."

Winn seized upon the phrase "old woman," successfully translating her homicidal feelings into mere indignation that a woman in her thirties would be called "old" by this young aristocratic snot. She thanked the Prophets for their gift from the mouth of Gul Ragat.

"Oh, I'm blathering. Let's return; Legate Migar probably wants to start the meeting again, and I don't want to be the last man back." He flashed her a boyish grin. "Could give him second thoughts about my *promotion*, what?"

PRESENT DAY

Kai Winn awoke in her bed, thirty years after the dream that had seemed so strong, so real. Am I that old, she asked herself, that I live in ancient memory instead of the present? Tomorrow is an important day, and I must rest.

The Kai rolled over, and was, thank the Prophets, dreamless for the rest of the night.

CHAPTER
1

CAPTAIN BENJAMIN SISKO stood in room 77A of the All Prophets Council chambers on Bajor, facing Kai Winn and surrounded by sixty-six vedeks and conciliators and priests and votaries and even an audience circumnavigating the viewing stage above the council floor. The crowd mobbed in from the left, circled the viewing stage, and exited on the opposite side, where their prayer tokens were collected. Major Kira Nerys stood next to the captain. As they had arranged, Kira spoke first.

"Most Gracious Kai," said Kira, "the Federation offers an . . . assignment of *Deep Space Nine* on a temporary basis, to Bajoran command."

Kai Winn frowned in the virtual council chambers, smoothing her plain frock. She pulled at one finger, carefully framing her reply in the most diplomatic terms possible. Although it was Kira who had spoken, she addressed her reply to Captain Sisko. "If the station remains under Federation control, Emissary, yet Shakar or some other member of the council becomes its governor, doesn't that mean we have accepted the authority of the Federation over Bajor?"

Damn her. Sisko—the "Emissary of the Prophets"—was careful to keep his poker face, but the Kai had a point. Tricky diplomacy was required not to offend the Bajorans. "The United Federation of Planets most certainly does *not* claim hegemony over Bajor, the council, or any vedek or political leader who might assume temporary control of the station."

Kai Winn shook her head; *"more in sorrow than anger,"* quoted Sisko silently to himself. "Emissary," she said, "if we control the station only subject to approval of our actions by the Federation Council, then we are nothing but puppets of the Federation." She put her hand over her mouth as if she had accidentally let slip an indiscretion. *Good acting job,* thought Sisko glumly. Kai Winn never did anything by accident. "I beg your pardon. . . . Perhaps it would be better to say we would be nothing but—political subsidiaries of the Federation. Rather like a colony or a protectorate."

Sisko took a deep breath. Winn had negotiated his back right up against a wall: he was authorized by the Federation Council to offer one further step . . . then that was it; if Kai Winn and the other vedeks didn't accept that offer, negotiations were at an end.

"The Federation is prepared to forgo the normal review process for turnovers of this sort in lieu of an explicit timeline of events, culminating with a final evaluation."

"You won't be looking over our shoulders? Emissary, how kind of you to make such an offer."

"No reviews until the final evaluation, Kai," added Kira, bobbing her head rapidly.

"But does the Emissary have the diplomatic authority to make such an offer?"

"I do," Sisko said. "And the Federation feels that with tensions between us and the Cardassians in abeyance for the moment, this would be an excellent time for such an experiment."

"How pleasant to carry on such productive negotiations." Kai Winn smiled broadly. *She's going to take it,* thought Sisko. And he was right: "I, too, am authorized by a vote of the leading vedeks of each party in the council to agree to the Federation offer—on a temporary basis, of course, subject to our own evaluation of the ongoing process."

Fancy footwork on first base to confuse the pitcher, thought Sisko with a simile. But the extra escape clause allowing Bajor to terminate the agreement early would not substantially alter the final proposal; the captain was certain the Federation Council would approve. "Then we have agreement, Kai Winn, Members of the Council. In nine days, you will send up a governor to assume control of *Deep Space Nine* for a period of sixty days . . . which may be extended indefinitely, provided both parties agree."

The Kai's eyes flickered toward First Minister Shakar when Sisko mentioned "governor." *An excellent choice,* thought the captain. Major Kira's only fear had been that Winn would try to take the position herself. For obvious reasons having little to do with the future of Bajor, Kira was quite pleased with the prospect of once again working under her old Resistance commander . . . and current romantic interest.

Before the final ceremony could begin, they were interrupted by the a chime of a combadge. Sisko tapped his combadge as discreetly as possible.

"Captain," Worf said, "My apologies for interrupting. But there is an urgent message for you from Starfleet. You are needed on *Deep Space Nine* at once."

"This had better be good," Sisko said to Worf under his breath. He was not looking forward to the explanations and apologies he'd have to give the council.

Back on the station, Kira was in no way pleased with the interruption from Starfleet. "Captain, couldn't whatever this message is have waited until we finished the negotiations or at least—"

"Let's see what Starfleet wants, Major. If it wasn't worth it, we'll soon know," Sisko said. As he spoke, he read down the text of the message on the padd that had been handed to him the moment he stepped into Ops.

"Sir, Kai Winn and the vedeks are going to be very upset. We walked right out on a meeting of the Council of All Prophets. . . . That's like—"

"Apparently a group of renegade Cardassians have invaded a star system on the edge of the Federation," Sisko said bluntly. "I think even Kai Winn and the vedeks will understand the urgency of the situation."

Kira froze in midsentence as the implication sank through her annoyance and humiliation and crash-landed on her comprehension circuits. If the Cardassians, any Cardassians, were starting a major offensive, the Federation was in grave danger, indeed—as was Bajor, needless to say. The Cardassians had never forgotten the embarrassment of Shakar and his compatriots forcing them off the only planet they never quite managed to subdue.

"How close?" she asked.

"Not very close, Major," said Worf, hovering nearby—*as usual when the subject is war,* thought Kira. "The Cardassians have invaded the system around Sierra-Bravo 112, the active half of the binary star system that includes the neutron star Stirnis."

The captain shook his head. "I was afraid of something like this; that's why I fought like the devil against this turnover of DS9. . . . At least right at this moment."

"Oh? And why is that?" She didn't mean it to sound quite so frosty; it was almost an autonomic reaction.

"I mean no slur against Bajor, Kira."

"I'm only concerned," he continued, "about the timing. While Starfleet is claiming that these Cardassians are renegades, disavowed by their central command, there could well be more to this. At the moment, I think it's a *terrible* idea to remove the Federation presence here."

"Radiation readings," said Dax, stepping forward from her science station, "in the vicinity of Sierra-Bravo 112 indicate a technological civilization on the second planet from the star, but the Federation long-range survey ship didn't pick up any subspace transmissions or warp signatures."

"Prime Directive, Old Man?" asked Sisko.

"Yes, Benjamin, I'm sure the Prime Directive would apply."

"Benjamin," continued Dax, "There are no enemy ships anywhere near here and a quarter of the Klingon fleet is on standby in case anything nasty comes out of the wormhole. Now is as good a time as any for the turnover—much as I hate to leave."

"Perhaps you're right," allowed Captain Sisko. "But in any case it's not an option: gentlemen, we have been ordered by Admiral Baang to at least investigate SB-112. . . . Investigate, not necessarily to act upon what we see. That, at least, Starfleet leaves to my discretion."

Kira's blood leapt in response to the simple

announcement—*stop! It's just another mission, it's nothing!* But her pulse raced regardless. The admiral had downplayed the potential for fighting, but Kira somehow *knew* the rumor would turn out to be true, and they would have no choice but to intervene. *And by the Prophets, I want to be on that job.* She tried to tell herself it was only to avoid tedious duty during the turnover . . . or even (a dark thought) to avoid the inevitable deep, meaningful discussion with Shakar about where they were headed—they, as in They.

But she was too honest to deny what she knew: she had killed Cardassians for so long—her whole adult life and much of her youth—that she had become accustomed to blood. She fought the dreams every waking moment and gave in to them at night   slinking once again through the black dark with disruptor rifle in arms, approaching the Cardassian sentry as quiet as a *meurik,* and "taking him out" (such euphemisms for perverse joy) with a k-bar knife.

Kira smiled, remembering grim and glorious days in the Shakaar resistance cell. "I can see where you're going to need someone like me, Captain." To go to battle again—against Cardassian aggression—was surely enough to overcome her conflicted desire to be with Shakar during his moment of triumph. *Besides,* she thought, putting a pious spin, *he'll be proud of my role in a mission like this.* It would mark the first time she went to war with Cardassian slavers on her own, without Shakar.

Sisko stopped, turning to gaze in seeming sereni-
ty upon the assembled senior crew, Kira in particular. "And that is why I am disappointed to have to
leave you behind, Major."

"What?" She blinked, not understanding.

"You are of course a very good choice for this
type of job, but you are the *only* person who can
smooth the inevitably choppy waters of the turnover of *Deep Space Nine* to the Bajoran government."

"But I—"

"Major Kira, when First Minister Shakar ar-
rives—or whoever is sent by the council—I cannot
give him an executive officer who is a member of
Starfleet; Kai Winn would never allow it. She's
already as nervous as a cat that this is a conspir-
acy to take away Bajor's independence. There are
only two people on the station she almost
trusts . . . and one of us, Major, has to command
the *Defiant.*"

Captain Sisko turned and ascended to his imper-
ial roost, leaving behind a Bajoran major with her
mouth opening and closing wordlessly. *But . . . I
should be in charge of the Cardassian operation!
Who else could—* Alas, when Kira turned for moral
support to the rest of the Ops crew, they had all
returned to their ongoing task to ready the station
for the turnover.

Kira blew a breath through her clenched teeth.
"Aye, sir," she said belatedly and angrily sat at her
station. *Don't be such a whiner,* she berated herself;

perhaps it's a hidden blessing from the Prophets. Leaving Kira as executive officer of the station not only provided stability, it would mean sixty days of face-to-face contact in a relationship that already appeared to be drifting toward the shoals of ne-glect. She smiled, wondering what it would be like to once again take orders from the most brilliant leader she had ever known.

CHAPTER
2

Two DAYS flickered past in the wink of an eye, but not without terrible yet vague foreshadowings of doom in Odo's imagination. The thought that he would probably be kept on by the Bajorans for a week or two, to facilitate in the turnover, before ultimately being let go, didn't calm him; just the reverse: if he couldn't stay on *Deep Space Nine* with Major Kira—and Kai Winn would never agree to any but a security officer who was Bajoran in descent as well as in name—Odo would much rather leave with Captain Sisko and these other people he had come to care for; *far better a strange posting with my friends.*

Odo would not admit it to himself except in the darkest moments of contemplation in his bucket, but he was frightened. Despite the physical appearance of a fully grown man, Odo was, in the long and short, less than fifteen years old; insecurity seized him, just as it had eight years earlier, when the Cardassians left and handed the station over to the unknown quantity of "The Federation." Odo felt as if he were learning the basic shapes all over again: cube, tetrahedron, pyramid, cylinder.

There was terribly much to do . . . so many things that could only be taken care of by Odo himself—and others requiring the personal attention of the captain or Dax or Worf—that departure on the *Defiant* to investigate the reports of Cardassian boojums was delayed for two days.

When at last everyone who was anyone (except for Kira) boarded the ship and prepared to cast off, leaving the rest of the packing-up and shipping-off to enlisted crew and sundry ensigns and "jaygees," Odo found himself staring out the window of the *Defiant* at the cold, silent station outside, as if it might be the last time he would ever see it again. *As well it might,* he told himself. *Now stop dithering and pull yourself together.* They would probably be returning, not to *Deep Space Nine,* but to another starbase and a detailing officer for new assignments . . . unless, against all odds, the Bajorans decided they didn't want the station after all, and they gave it back in sixty days. (If the Federation *took* it back, over Bajoran wishes, Odo decided glumly, it would cause a quadrantwide diplomatic incident.)

In the four years Odo had known the captain, he had learned to read the man, and Sisko was, if anything, even more agitated than the constable. Captain Sisko paced on the bridge, something he never did, and he snarled at Dax when the lieutenant commander tried to tell him what a great job he'd done as CO on the station. "You're already writing my obituary," said the captain quietly— not quietly enough. He sat in his command chair with a loud thump.

Dax took the drastic events with more equanimity, which didn't surprise Odo in the least; in all her lifetimes, she must have been uprooted and sent to Outer Nowhere more times than she could count. She probably no longer even felt nervous or lonely in new places. *Or perhaps she's just better at hiding her feelings,* he thought. But Dr. Bashir sat white-faced and white-knuckled in the supernumerary jump seat; *Deep Space Nine,* Odo knew, had been Bashir's very first posting after leaving Starfleet Academy—his first and only Starfleet home. He was as nervous as a Ferengi on trial about what might lie ahead—not on Sierra-Bravo, not for *Deep Space Nine,* but in his own life and career. Worf and Chief O'Brien were stoical; but then, they had only recently arrived from some Starfleet ship, and Worf would never show his nervousness anyway. *The chief will at least bring his family along,* the constable realized.

Curiously enough, Odo decided he would even miss Quark. *Well . . . perhaps a little; I'll miss the relentless games and contests—games I always won.* But Odo sighed, realizing he was only fooling himself; over many years and too many near-death experiences to count, he had come to hold a grudging respect for that one particular Ferengi. And he suspected that Quark, who would be even more reluctant to admit it to himself, would miss Odo every bit as much.

Commander Dax ran through the departure checklist: "Check balast. . . . Nav systems on-line and operational. . . . Weapons and shields within operational capacities. . . . Level-three diagnostics nominal. . . . Doctor? Doctor Bashir? *Defiant* bridge to Doctor Bashir." The doctor jumped up with a strangled noise and darted to the nearest console. "Infirmary—I mean, sickbay diagnostics nominal; no problems detected."

Odo listened to the pulse of departure, all the routine tasks that junior officers struggled over, but which the senior crew now aboard could do in their sleep. The sounds were familiar, not quite as comforting as reading the daily incident reports in his security office, but better than standing and staring out the porthole.

"Dax," began the captain, "what have you found out about Sierra-Bravo 112 from the planetary database?"

"Hm? Oh, it's a six-planet system, but only 112-II is of any real interest. The inner planet is a burned-out hulk of nickle-iron; the outer four are gas giants.

"112-II has a technological civilization at least capable of broad-spectrum EM transmission. . . . No warp signatures detected in the three sweeps on ultra-long-range scanners, but that was eighty years ago. Spectroscopic analysis indicates it's extraordinarily rich in latinum, selenium, and trilithium-disulphite."

Odo interrupted. "Which cannot be easily separated into dilithium, as I recall."

"On the nose, Constable." Dax continued. "There are atmospheric traces of cyanide, so there's probably some cyanide compound in the local life-forms."

"Doctor Bashir," queried the captain, "should we have to beam down, can you protect the away team from the level of cyanide in the atmosphere? And can we eat the local food?"

Odo watched the doctor poke at his console, transferring Dax's data entry to his own station. "Well, yes and no, sir: yes, a simple hypospray can counter the level of poison residue on the atmospheric dust, but no, we surely cannot eat the local food."

"Then it's com-rations all the way," said Sisko with a smile.

There was a sudden and urgent pounding on the airlock door; everybody on the bridge jumped and stared except for the captain. Sisko closed his eyes and let his head fall back on his command chair. "Who is that rapping at my chamber door?" He did not sound pleased that his final departure from the station had been marred by such an unseemly occurrence.

Worf looked back and forth, twice, between Sisko and the door; the infernal racket started up again, sounding to Odo as if some persistent neighbor were beating on the airlock with a battering ram. Odo moved to the airlock and cycled it open.

Standing before him was an aggrieved and very noisy Quark. "Don't tell me you simply *forgot* to let me in on the departure time," whined the Ferengi.

"Forgot? Quark, I never forget anything. Let me assure you, the snub was quite deliberate."

"Captain—I appeal to you in the name of . . . of kindly benevolence. These *people* who are taking the station over are absolutely impossible. They haven't the first idea of how a free market should work—believe me, I know. I've tried to open a franchise on Bajor for the past—"

"You mean," interrupted Constable Odo, interpreting for the captain, "you've been trying to palm off your stolen merchandise, but the Bajorans are too moral and ethical to deal in contraband." Odo crouched low to stare directly into Quark's eyes; he was gratified to see the felonious Ferengi lose his train of thought.

But Quark quickly rallied. "Not in the least, Captain Sisko. I have legitimate business interests in the sector you're headed toward. . . ."

Odo was on a roll; Quark couldn't seem to open his mouth without convicting himself. "Really,

Quark? And just how do *you* know where we're headed? That information is classified."

The Ferengi managed to look innocently surprised. "Aren't you going to the binary pair of the neutron star Stirnis? I heard through the grapevine—"

"There is no grapevine, Quark; the information was classified. And I suppose you're going to deny tapping into the station computers?"

"Odo! That would be illegal." Quark grinned, exposing a full, snaggly set of freshly sharpened teeth. "Captain, I just want to come along with you. I can't stand all this . . . *religion.*" He shuddered, glancing back over his shoulder.

Odo stretched both hands out and gripped the sides of the airlock door, expanding his arms into a nice imitation of a thorny thicket. "Captain, I strongly advise against allowing this . . . unindicted co-conspirator to accompany us."

Dax wormed her way past an exasperated Worf and stood next to the constable. "Oh, come now, Odo. Would you rather leave this unindicted co-conspirator alone on the station to work his magic while you're gone for *at least* two weeks?"

Odo said nothing at first; then the full horror of the lieutenant commander's point became clear to him. Quark, alone on the station, with nothing but Bajoran religious figures to control him. . . . Quark *running amok.*

"I believe Dax has you there, Constable," said

the captain; he almost sounded as though he were smirking. "The real question is, are you selfish enough to wish Quark on the rest of the station just so you, personally, won't have to deal with him?"

The blow slid home like the well-aimed thrust of a Klingon *d'k tahg*. "No, I . . . I suppose I'm not," mumbled Odo, feeling thrice a fool, three times over. Glumly, he retracted his thickets; after a moment spent in a glaring contest with Quark, Odo stepped aside and allowed the Ferengi to enter.

"Thank you," said Quark, with a shirty sort of exaggerated politeness; he rolled his eyes as he passed the constable. "Really, imagine trying to hog all that latinum for yourselves."

It took a moment to sink in. "Latinum? Quark, *how did you know* about the latinum? You *did* break into the Federation planetary database! That's a class-two felony. . . . Captain, I must insist—"

"Odo, Odo, Odo," said Quark, shaking his head sadly. "I'm shocked, shocked that you have never heard the Ferengi legends of, ah, the Grand Planet of Latinum, fabled in Ferengi lore. Have you?"

"No, Quark," said the constable, curling his lip, so close, he could almost taste the charge . . . and the Ferengi was in danger of slithering away again. "I've never heard of a 'Grand Planet of Latinum,' and neither have you! There is no such legend."

The Ferengi made a grand theatrical gesture. "Why, every Ferengi knows it lies in, why, right there in Sierra-Bravo 112. When I heard where you were going, I just knew I had to explore . . . for Ferenginar—for the Grand Nagus, not for myself."

"Every Ferengi?" demanded Odo, making himself bigger. "So if I were to ask, say, Nog—"

"Ah, youth! Young Ferengi are so poorly educated these days, and I'm afraid my ignorant nephew is even less assiduous about it than most."

Odo opened and closed his mouth, feeling as a starving solid must feel when food is dangled, then snatched cruelly away. But once again, Quark had beaten the charge. The constable snorted and turned away, frustrated.

"All *aboard,*" sang out Chief O'Brien; it was evidently some obscure Federation reference, and Odo didn't catch it. Snorting heavily, Worf poked at the door panel with a meaty forefinger, and the airlock slid shut.

"Are we all done now?" inquired Captain Sisko, looking directly at the constable.

"I, uh, don't think there will be any more interruptions," muttered Odo, still struggling to find the flaw in Quark's ridiculous fabrication. Great Planet of Latinum!

"Thank you. Cast off, Old Man; let's really wring out this beautiful piece of machinery. Who knows? It may be our last time."

With a wistful-sounding "aye, aye," Dax ran the final launch checklist, detached the *Defiant* from her moorings, turned a sharp 130 degrees, and headed off toward the star system known only as

Sierra-Bravo 112. Odo watched Quark as if the Ferengi might shoplift a warp coil.

The days crawled with exaggerated slowness for Major Kira Nerys as she nervously awaited Shakar's arrival. She paced the long, crowded corridors in the habitat ring, sidestepping the hundreds of boxes and antigrav dollies, dancing around civilian and Starfleet movers, and occasionally studying some transitioning resident's requisition without really seeing what she saw. She really had too much to do herself to waste time wandering the rest of the station; every security code and classified program in Ops had to be either changed to Bajoran standards or encrypted and hidden away, in case the "temporary" turnover really did turn out to be temporary.

Secretly, in her heart, Kira suspected that was the most likely outcome. *I guess I really don't think we're quite ready yet,* she thought, feeling strangely ambivalent where she ought to feel either patriotic pride in Bajor's accomplishments or burning shame at the places where they fell short. But having sat through more than her share of Bajoran council meetings and seen, firsthand, the astonishing acrimony over the slightest miscommunication or dispute, she was sure the Federation had been wise to slip in the sixty-day escape clause.

Am I just being an unpatriotic snob? What, Bajor's not "good enough" because we're not the wonderous, omnipotent FEDERATION? The thought truly bothered her, as did what it implied about her lack of confidence in Shakar, but there it was with all its humiliating consequences: *I truly believe we're just not ready and this whole turnover is going to be a fiasco.*

What was worse, Kira was ninety percent certain that Kai Winn was setting Shakar up to fail; and the Kai would use his so-called "failure" as a hammer to bludgeon him out of his post as First Minister. "Beware, Shakar; Winn has always wanted *exclusive power* in the hands of the vedeks," spoke Kira into a letter log she planned to send down to Shakar before he departed for the station.

But she knew it was to no avail; if Winn offered the governorship to Shakar, there was no way he could refuse it without appearing weak and losing face. That, too, might cost him his ministerial rank. Shakar would just have to take his chances; maybe, against all the odds, he could succeed so well that the turnover would become permanent.

Kira finished the letter log and encrypted it using the special, one-way key code she and Shakar used. (It was definitely the sort of undiplomatic missive one didn't want falling into the "wrong hands," especially the Council of Vedeks.) Then she sent it with a request for receipt confirmation. The major waited for fifteen minutes near the console, but there was no friendly double beep; evidently, Shakar was not available to hear it right away.

Odo's office was immaculate, of course; he had

not packed up anything, since there was still a reasonable chance that the Bajorans would keep him on as internal security officer, or "constable." Kira had made a persuasive case that Odo could enforce Bajoran social-religious law as easily as he could Federation law . . . or for that matter, the harsh Cardassian legislative code of *Terek Nor,* though she still wasn't quite sure he appreciated her efforts. Still, because it was a good time to do it—Captain Sisko would need a full legal accounting for his final outprocessing report—Kira wanted to perform a complete inventory of all cases handled, their dispositions, active and ongoing investigations, informant lists, and profiles of "suspicious characters," as Odo termed them (by whatever arcane methods he used to arrive at that determination). Odo would have done it himself, of course; it was just the sort of nitpicky thing that Odo loved and the major detested. But he was away on the *Defiant,* and the task fell to her.

She started setting up the query criteria for the computer, similar to an engineering diagnostic scan but for security office actions rather than computer responses. She yawned several times . . . and then blinked her eyes, confused, feeling the warm, smooth press of Odo's desk against her cheek. It took Kira several seconds to realize she had actually *fallen asleep* at her task, and more than an hour had passed.

Jumping up with a confused start, she stared wildly around; the computer beeped, and Kira realized that was what had awakened her in the first place. "Attention Major Kira," said the smooth female voice, "runabout from Bajor docking at Docking Bay Four, carrying the new governor of *Deep Space Nine.*"

"Shakar!" *So that's why he never acknowledged my message; he was already en route.* Kira headed for the door but had to stop halfway and squat onto her hams to avoid passing out. When her blood pressure climbed back to "awake" level, she jogged to the nearest turbolift, which hauled her out to the habitat ring, up the pylon, and into the docking bay. She straightened her uniform and only belatedly realized that she was the only person in the reception area not in dress uniform. When the huge airlock door rolled aside on its geared teeth, she felt a flush of embarrassment creep up her neck to her cheeks and nose ridges. If only she hadn't stupidly fallen asleep, she could have greeted the First Minister with the proper ritual. Her cheek still felt creased from Odo's desk.

The inner airlock and the door of the runabout rolled back simultaneously in opposite directions, and a mob of diplomatic-looking Bajorans shuffled out, murmuring ritualized greetings and well-wishes.

Then the mob parted, and a large gentleman—a vedek Kira didn't know—stepped up to her. "Major? May I present the credentials of the new governor of *Deep Space Nine,* now called *Emissary's Sanctuary.*"

The vedek stepped aside, and a small, plump and frumpy woman stepped forward with grave dignity and a phony, ingratiating smile. "Hello, my child," said Kai Winn, beaming. "May the peace of the Prophets be with you always."

Kira forgot every word of the wonderful speech she had prepared. She stared in horror at her new boss for the next sixty days . . . *or maybe forever.* "I . . . I . . . hi, Kai." Then she flushed even harder. "The, ah, station greets you, my Kai; may the peace of the Prophets be on you. Be *with* you. This is so . . . so—"

"Unexpected?" suggested Kai Winn with a toothy smile. It wasn't exactly the word Major Kira had in mind.

CHAPTER
3

THIS IS *a bad dream,* thought Major Kira. *Any minute now, I'll wake up and—*

Kira sat up suddenly in bed, head spinning like a gyroscopic stabilizing unit. She had been having a nightmare: Kai Winn fired everybody in *Deep Space Nine,* even the Bajorans, and replaced them with corpses and monsters reanimated by black magic.

The reality wasn't much different, except instead of the walking dead, the Kai was in the process of replacing all the longtime administrative personnel on the station with her own cadre . . . what Kira insisted upon thinking of as the Kai's "toadies." Although the top officers of *Deep Space Nine* were all Starfleet (hence, leaving anyway), the women and men who did much of the day-to-day "real" work were civilians: the janitors, dockwallopers, communications and traffic controllers, ship inspectors, security personnel, jailers, tour guides, lawyers and paralegals, maintenance workers, astronomers, fuel handlers, painters, and polishers. None of these people was actually *required* by Starfleet to leave when the Federation pulled off the station, and since most of them were Bajorans, Kira had simply assumed that Kai Winn would keep them in their jobs.

No such luck. The Kai arrived in the airlock with sixteen bags of personal effects and a forty-screen list of patrons who had supported her bid to jump from vedek to Kai. Kira stood next to Kai Winn, still blinking pieces of sleep out of her eyes and desperately wishing for another coffee, and highlighted names on the list as they showed up at the station. The docking pylons had become huge traffic snarls, jammed with resentful members of the newly disemployed shuffling out and down, to be replaced by smug and fervent boosters of Kai Winn cycling up and in.

The major's only consolation, as she broke up the third fight that morning—a laid-off gardener with two children tried to plant a geranium in the skull of a childless, unmarried lay pastor who had just taken his job—was that Kai Winn was setting herself up for a spectacular failure. . . . After which, with Winn disgraced, surely the Council of

Vedeks would reconsider the only other obvious candidate for governor . . . First Minister Shakar.

The lay pastor's head turned out to be much harder than his attacker anticipated; Constable Odo was away on the mission to Sierra-Bravo; Kai Winn was far too busy to worry about minor details like assault and battery; the holding cells were already full to overflowing; and to tell the truth, Major Kira's sympathies lay entirely with the gardener. There was nothing to do but scream at the attacker for several minutes and send him on his way.

The major was just pushing the subdued family man onto the runabout, which would take him down to Bajor and a long stint in the Office of Labor Resource Allocation, waiting for another job opening, when the stupidity of what Kira had been doing for the past few days hit her square in the conscience. She turned away, mumbling a long string of blasphemies against the Kai through clenched teeth, and discovered herself nose to nose with Kai Winn.

The Kai smiled ingratiatingly. "Child, what troubles you? Do you worry about the justice of removing so many people, even Bajorans, from their jobs?"

"Kai!" Kira stared, dithering between keeping her job and keeping her sanity; sanity won. "Well . . . now that you mention it, yes. Why are you doing this? What have these people ever done to deserve . . ." Kira groped for the word. "To deserve *exile?*"

"Exile? No one is being exiled, child. They are all welcome to stay." Kai Winn gestured expansively, evidently including the entire station. "If these Bajorans wish to begin taking more seriously the traditions and spiritual beliefs of our people, they may even be given new jobs here on the *Emissary's Sanctuary.*"

"Big of you." Kira struggled in vain to keep the sarcasm out of her voice.

Kai Winn shook her head sadly. "They have made their choices, child; those who choose to live by the secular law alone, not according to the ancient wisdom of the Prophets, have only those rights protected by the law: which means, my child, I can let them go whenever I decide others should take their places."

Isn't there anyplace in the heart of a Kai for *compassion?* Kira thought, and for a moment wondered if she had spoken aloud. But if Kai Winn heard anything, she chose not to take offense; she merely smiled and repeated the justification that those being "let go" were the purely secular workers who were either not devoted enough to the Prophets . . . or at least not public enough in their devotions and rituals.

"Fine. Just fine—my Kai." *Then I should be the first one fired,* Kira thought as she squeezed her fists, fingernails stabbing painfully into her palms; *and where the hell were YOU when we "seculars"*

*were fighting Cardassia to give you back your bloody
world?* Fortunately, the major left the latter unsaid.

"No, Major Kira," said the Kai with the same
smug, irritating smile, "you are still needed. For
reasons I cannot discuss, I must retain you in your
position as executive officer of *Emissary's Sanctuary.*"

Kai Winn put her hand on Kira's head, murmuring a blessing; then she walked away, already
having forgotten the major's outburst . . . and the
very real concerns that sparked it.

*She doesn't understand that the turnover is just a
temporary measure,* thought Kira, amazed; *does
she really think it's going to be PERMANENT?* The
major's next thought was even more chilling: *What
if she has a plan I don't know about?*

The Federation ordered the turnover to see how
well the Bajorans could adapt to running a full-
sized starbase, a "coming-of-age" test to see how
mature Bajor was after decades of Cardassian
occupation. Kira had always told herself that after
the sixty days, everything would revert to normal.
But Kai Winn was a Very Imporant Life-Form in
the Federation recently . . . and if the Kai absolutely insisted on keeping the station, would Starfleet risk an interstellar incident by insisting on
taking it back? In fact, who was to say the Kai
hadn't already worked it out (at a level far above
Captain Sisko) that Bajor would keep the station,
no matter what the agreement read?

For the first five days of Kai Winn's tenure (of either sixty days or forever), Kira's anger and jumpiness increased exponentially. She followed the Kai around like a pet *dakthara,* taking dictated orders and being sent to tell families that their fates were now in limbo: they were being removed from positions they had held, quite literally, since *Deep Space Nine* had been *Terek Nor.* By the end of the transition period, as the last of Kai Winn's "toadies" was ensconced in a job that used to be considered critical but now was just patronage, Kira had developed a burning itch to beam the Kai into empty space. The major had just begun to envision the infuriating old woman gasping for a lungful of nonexistent air when she realized what a blasphemy even such a thought was. Kira forcibly erased all violent thoughts from her mind; she was more religious than she generally liked to let on, even to herself.

She sat in her normal chair up in Ops, all alone, feeling as if she were the one who had moved to a new duty station; instead, it had been quite literally everyone else who had abandoned her. The patrons of the Kai who had been placed on Ops duty rotation—every one a brother, sister, or an ordained sub-vedek—were far too busy "administrating," whatever that meant, actually to stand their watches; they never showed up, leaving Kira to do the work of four people.

It hardly mattered. The stationwide com-channel chimed, catching Kira's attention. The

Kai's beaming visage appeared on the main screen—a prerecorded message, Kira guessed. "Good day, my children. I know how hard it must be for you to adjust to your new duties. The ears of Bajor have heard your heartfelt pleas. . . . Until this trying turnover is complete, Bajor, in my person, hereby bars all ships' traffic with *Emissary's Sanctuary*. For the moment, until we stand aright again, we Bajorans must concern ourselves only with Bajor; the outside world must wait."

"Excellent idea," muttered Kira, making sure no "ears of Bajor" were stretched nearby. "Who needs the sector, the quadrant, the entire Federation when we can stick our heads in a hole instead?" *Surely we couldn't be invaded TWICE!*—but she kept the last thought silent.

"In keeping with this new focus," continued the smug smile of Bajor, "each must concentrate him or herself on the inner soul. There are a number of old customs and laws from the bright days before the Occupation that must be restored, if Bajor is to be once again Bajoran. A complete list shall be available on the main computers and will also be posted on bulkheads in the Promenade, in accordance with the ancient custom."

"By All the Prophets," breathed a stunned Kira, "are we going to revive the old laws?" She stared at her hands, hands that had about as much chance of becoming great sculptors as Kai Winn had of winning a Ferengi beauty contest.

Frantic, the major poked at the panel before her, calling up the file. It took a moment to find; she finally tried "Code of the Prophets," and the list appeared.

It wasn't as long as she'd thought it would be . . . and it did *not* include certain archaic provisions that she had feared—*praise the Prophets and the Kai's mercy!* But as Kira read each law, most of which she had never seen before, her mouth opened in astonishment. "Rank? Seniority? Etiquette between boys and girls? This is a military code." When she reached the detailed passages about food preparation, incense burning, hair length—she fingered her own too-short hair, wondering whether the executive officer of *Emissary's Sanctuary* would be forced to grow locks down to her shoulders—she sat back, more amused than angry. "Yeah, good luck, my Kai."

Kira met Kai Winn on the Promenade. "Child," said the Kai, "there is one den of iniquity that I'm sure you'll be pleased to see converted to more, shall we say, appropriate uses?"

Kira thought for a moment, but really, the reference was clear. "You mean Quark's Place?"

Winn leaned close. "It's not just that it serves liquor," she whispered, glancing left and right conspiratorially; Kira followed suit automatically. "Child, you cannot be aware of what dreadful debauchery lurks in the upper chambers."

"Oh, you mean the . . ." Kira stopped; if the Kai

thought she hadn't known about the holosuites, why disabuse her? "You mean the other Dabo tables?"

Kai Winn shuddered, marking the sign of the Prophets upon her ample belly. She took Kira's arm, clumsily wrenching the major's elbow painfully. "You don't want to know, child; truly, thank the Prophets you were in ignorance! But now that the—*Ferengi*—will be leaving, we must decide what to do with the space. And we must inspect the premises now, painful as that may be.

"Let your moral code guide you," prayed the Kai, "and walk hand in hand with the Prophets."

Rom, who was looking after the bar while Quark himself was mercifully away with the *Defiant*, instantly busied himself monkeying around with the glassware. His hands shook, and he clinked the glasses hard enough to break one, leading Major Kira to the conclusion Rom was very much aware that almost everything about Quark's was a violation of the Code. The Ferengi didn't even glance up as Kira and the Kai entered, clinching the case, but Kira decided to keep her mouth shut, hoping the Kai was too preoccupied to notice.

"Rom!" shouted Kira, trying to alert him. *"Two root beers. Kai Winn, you have to try this drink!"*

The Kai declined and headed out quickly. Kira hurried on behind the blithely indifferent Winn as she bustled out of the erstwhile bar and headed into the Promenade; the Kai set a straight line for the turbolift, ignoring the swarms of the devout who parted around her like waves before a ship. Kai Winn enunciated a firm "Operations" to the computer, and the lift obediently began to rise.

Dog's breakfast, that's what Chief O'Brien would have said; this whole experiment is turning into a real dog's breakfast. Kira should have exulted: the station in an uproar, positions filled by incompetent political hacks, ancient religious codes forced upon reluctant residents . . . surely all this nonsense would lead to the complete disgrace of Kai Winn and her entire faction.

The major almost smiled, but she didn't feel like smiling; instead, she felt a great sadness that Bajor had been given a chance and was throwing it away in a futile effort to recapture the glory days of the Prophets instead of moving into the modern century.

"Dog's breakfast," said Kira with conviction.

"I'm sorry, my child, I don't understand."

"It's something Chief O'Brien says."

"Oh, yes. Colorful man. What does it mean?"

Kira shrugged. "Oh, I can't really say." *Not QUITE a lie,* she told herself. The turbolift hummed for Ops, carrying the Kai to the very office once occupied by the Emissary, and before him, by Gul Dukat, as he oversaw the enslavement of the world.

"A pig's breakfast," said Chief O'Brien, reading the scanners over Dax's shoulder. "A real pig's breakfast."

The Trill science officer looked back at the chief. "What exactly *do* pigs eat for breakfast?"

The chief didn't answer the question, at least not literally.

"Seven Cardassian warships, Captain," he added. "Couple of heavies, GM-class, a cruiser, and the other four are speeder-destroyers. Identification shows they were all reported stolen over the last two years."

"So they may well be renegades," Sisko said, "or perhaps Cardassian Central Command is looking for plausible deniability. Chief, what odds would you give us?"

"If we popped off the cloak and opened fire? Well, we might cripple one of the GMs in the first volley, then the other would engage us, and the destroyers would nibble us to death."

"Wouldn't advise it?"

"No, sir. Not if you're wanting to make it away in one piece. And frankly, sir, I wouldn't advise revealing our presence for any reason . . . not even to send a diplomatic message for them to bug out."

The captain stroked his beard; "I don't like this," he said to Dax. "I don't like sitting here doing *nothing.*"

"Then we'd better get down to the planet ourselves, Benjamin," she replied. *Amen to that,* thought O'Brien. . . . Then he remembered the odds: seven Cardassian warships could mean as many as fifteen hundred soldiers on the ground.

Odo stepped off the turbolift onto the bridge, fresh after several hours spent in his bucket.

O'Brien watched the constable narrowly; Odo frowned and scowled, clasped his hands behind his back, and made other fidgety signs that he wasn't satisfied. The chief decided information was more important than secrecy. "Captain, I'd like to make a full level-three scan of the entire system."

"Chief, wait," said Jadzia Dax, "the Cardassians can detect level three. . . . Maybe we'd better make it level two."

"That won't tell us enough, Commander." As usual, O'Brien found himself annoyed when he had to argue with a commissioned officer; he always had the sneaking suspicion that he was starting several points down already. "Level three will show us any technology hidden on the second planet. We can't rely on the lack of ships."

"And the Cardassians?" asked Sisko.

"I'm hoping they're too preoccupied with suppressing the planet to pay that much attention to their passive sensors."

Sisko nodded absently; surprised at winning so easily, O'Brien quickly completed the scan before the captain could change his mind. The systems chief stared at the viewer as the readout slowly crawled across the screen; his mouth opened wider with every pass.

Dax, crowding the screen, said, "What are you . . . oh. Wow."

"Well?" demanded the constable. "Is there any hidden technology on the planet?"

"Well, Odo, I really can't say," said O'Brien.

"And why not?" The changeling looked even more annoyed than usual.

The chief snorted. "Because I can't read a sundial under a spotlight."

Everyone on the bridge except for Dax stared at the chief. "You're going to have to explain that last one," said the captain.

If he's upset now, just wait until he sees the report. "I mean, sir, I'm not sure whether we're going to rescue the life-forms on this planet . . . or vice versa," said O'Brien.

"Thank you, Chief," Odo said, "now perhaps you'd care to explain your explanation?"

"In short, simple sentences," added Sisko, articulating each word distinctly.

"What he means, Benjamin," Dax put in, "is that there's so much technology on that planet—technology far beyond anything the Cardassians have, or us either—that there's no possible way to tell if there's anything unusual; it would be lost in the glare."

"And *that,*" said O'Brien in triumph, pointing at the viewer, "is what a pig eats for breakfast."

CHAPTER
4

Jadzia Dax hunched down at her console so everybody could peer over her head at the viewer. "Yes," she said, "I'd say this qualifies as a porcine meal, Chief."

Sisko voiced the thought on everyone's mind . . . certainly on Dax's. "I don't think I've ever seen so much technology in one place. And what technology! I can't even begin to guess what half of it does. . . . But why haven't they warned away the Cardassians yet?"

Dax noticed something and moved to shift the scan frequencies, but Bashir's elbow was in the way. "Julian J. Bashir, *do you mind?*"

He jumped away from her instruments. "J? What does the J stand for?"

"You don't want to know," muttered the Trill, readjusting to scan for life-forms. "Um . . . well, looks like there's life on that planet, all right."

"How many species?" interrupted Bashir.

"Hm." Jadzia Dax ran a quick subroutine. "About three million, Julian. Mostly insects, I'd guess."

Bashir gave her a look. "I mean how many sentient species, as if you didn't know."

"One. Wait, I take that back: there are actually three. . . . Cardassian, Drek'la, and an unknown— presumably the natives of the planet. There are about a dozen Cardassians, a thousand Drek'la, and eleven million natives."

"Drek'la?" Sisko asked. "Never heard of them."

"Me neither," Dax said, "let me check the records. Here they are. They're a space-living race, very small in numbers. That thousand of them must be a good percentage of their entire species. They're like hermit crabs, stealing and/or recovering old spaceships and using them as home."

"Interesting. Are they working for the Cardassians, or did they capture the Cardassians along with their ships? And just eleven million of the natives on the entire planet?"

"Yes, pretty sparse. There are quite a few cities, but they're mostly deserted, except Cardassians occupy two of them. The indigenous population is sticking to the countryside. No subspace or radio communications, no space presence."

"But that's *it.*" The chief suddenly stood, staring at the forward viewer; he paced right up to it, so close he was probably looking at individual pixels. Dax waited patiently; Chief O'Brien continued. "Captain, that's the explanation for everything: these eleven million creatures must be the degenerated remnants of the mighty civilization that built all this technology. They probably don't even know how to use it anymore."

"I hate to say it," said Quark from across the room, "but the chief's got a pretty good explanation."

"When did *he* sneak in here?" demanded Odo, but no one answered.

"It would explain why they don't just zap the Cardassians—or Drek'la or whoever—out of orbit," concluded Quark.

"Let's not jump to conclusions. Dax, is there any sign of resistance? Weapons discharge, explosions, fires, battle lines?"

Dax scanned from pole to pole, letting the planet revolve beneath the *Defiant,* whose orbit was high enough, forty-two thousand kilometers, that they were only moving at half the angular velocity of the planetary rotation. "Nope; nothing on this side. The Drek'la and a few Cardassians are filling up the cities, the natives are going about their business in the countryside."

"As if they weren't even aware they'd been invaded," mused the captain. "All right, Dax;

throw an away team together. Starfleet Command and I want to know what's going on down there."

Dax stood, slipping out from the knot of players to decide who would accompany her downstairs. *Worf, obviously; O'Brien to evaluate their technology; hm . . . oh, of course: Odo for infiltrations.* "You, you, you—volunteers. Meet me in transporter room three in ten. Oh, Worf, where do you keep the planetary exploration-survival gear? And weapons; there are enemies about."

Quark spoke up unexpectedly. "Commander Dax, if you don't have any objection, I'd like to be on the away team."

Quark? QUARK?

"Well, Dax may have no objection," snarled Odo, "but I certainly do."

Quark shook his head sadly and spoke to Dax. "I suppose he just has a problem dealing with any authority but his own. Especially female authority, poor fellow. If you choose to have me—I mean, have me along—I don't see how it's any decision of his; after all, the captain did put *you* in charge."

Dax chuckled; she knew exactly what Quark was doing. He made the same mistake everyone did: assuming Jadzia *Dax* was as young and easily charmed as Jadzia might have been (though in truth, Dax didn't think even the prejoined Jadzia had been all that innocent and naive a girl). On the other hand, Dax did not have quite the same knee-jerk reaction against Ferengi capitalists as did most Starfleet officers, who believed that the Federation had long since "transcended" such "destructive competition." As an alliance of traders, the Ferengi would deal with everyone . . . which meant they had to learn to deal with anyone. Necessity had given them an uncanny ability to penetrate right to the heart of unknown cultures and civilizations—and figure out what they could be talked into buying.

"Thanks for volunteering, Quark; glad to have you aboard." Odo opened his mouth, but Dax interrupted before he could say a word. "Get down to the transporter and try not to kill Quark before we make planetfall."

Less than ten minutes later, everyone stood on the transporter pads wearing backpacks with enough equipment to climb Mount Traxanaxanos on Betazed (a task which Torias Dax had actually tried three times before giving up in disgust). A transporter chief waited patiently for the order to energize.

Bashir went to each away team member in turn and hyposprayed him in the neck. "There are trace particulates in the air that are poisonous," he explained. "This should protect you. But you'd better perform a complete microbioscan of anything local you want to eat or drink; a single hypospray can't protect you from large doses."

"Hit us," said Dax, pointing at the woman; after a moment's hesitation, the transporter chief ran her fingers down the transporter touchplate. The next thing Dax saw was the side of a mountain, appropriately enough; they were standing on the slope, looking down into a verdant valley dotted with small hamlets.

She turned and did a slow scan with her tricorder. "Well, one direction's as good as another, I suppose," said the Trill. "Let's head down that way." She set out toward the nearest hamlet, setting a brisk pace that would get them to their destination in just over half an hour. The Cardassians were a hundred klicks away, not moving at the moment.

The plant life was lush, but everything had a peculiar bluish tint; Dax scanned the vegetation carefully as she passed it: in addition to a form of chlorophyll, the plants also contained peculiar trace elements. "Cynanine," she reported, "and a lot of radical cyanogens."

"What does that mean?" asked Worf.

"It means the doctor was right: please don't eat the grass. We'll have to pack our lunch."

"The food is poisonous? To Cardassians and Drek'la as well?"

"Well, I'm sure the Natives enjoy the spice. Yes, Worf, poisonous to Cardassians and Drek'la too."

O'Brien spoke up. "So what would they be wanting with the planet, then? They can't live here; they can't colonize the place."

Quark was on hands and knees; at first Dax thought he had stumbled, but he was examining something on the ground. "That's an excellent question, Chief," she said. "It's been noted and logged. But at the moment, I don't have a clue why."

"Well, I think I do," muttered Quark; he began to slither on the ground, sniffing at the dirt. "Looks like that Starfleet database—I mean the Ferengi legends were actually *right.*" He continued rooting along the soil like a worm.

"Oh, please," said Odo, rolling his eyes in disgust. "I've half a mind to change into a *verlak* bird and swallow you whole."

Quark looked up at the constable. "Well, you're definitely right about one thing."

"Oh? And what's that?"

"You have half a mind."

"Gentlemen, please. Now what did you just say, Quark?"

The Ferengi stood up, brushing off his painfully colorful knickers and vest. "Oh, nothing. Never mind."

But Dax was wise to the ways of Ferengi. She pointed her tricorder at the dirt. "Interesting," she exclaimed. "The soil is saturated with latinum drops."

Quark stared mesmerized at the ground. "There must be . . . thousands of bars, just waiting to be siphoned up. . . ."

Quark's nose was right; but latinum was the least of the riches: tiny dilithium crystals were also liberally scattered through the soil, as were eleven other rare minerals. "The Ferengi Alliance would die for the mining rights," remarked Dax.

"Hey, I saw it first," wailed Quark. He dropped to his knees and spread his arms protectively over the ground. "I claim this dirt in the name of Quark's Mining and Mineral Processing Facility."

Odo snorted and pointed an accusing finger, stretching it a full meter to wag directly in the Ferengi's face. "You have no mining and mineral-processing facility."

"I do now," responded Quark defensively.

"It belongs to the Federation, not to you and your Nagus."

"Look, I don't mean to interrupt," said Chief O'Brien, "but this planet already *has* eleven million owners. If anyone owns it, they do."

Dax smiled. "Anyone who wants the mining rights will have to find something the Natives want more and negotiate for it."

"That can be arranged," added Quark, still sullen at being denied his claim. "If necessary," he added under his breath.

"But at least," continued the Trill, "we have a pretty good idea why the Cardassians and Drek'la are here. And that means they're not likely to just pack up and leave." *Dax,* she imagined Benjamin saying, *if you say "this place is a gold mine," your away team is going to mutiny.* She wrinkled her nose—even she could smell the metallic tang of latinum.

While everyone else mulled over the fortune they were standing on, Dax decided to change the subject. She recalibrated the field variables on her tricorder and did another sweep. "I really, really don't like being surrounded by tons of technology, and I mean literally tons, that I don't have a clue about. The stuff is just lying around, unattended." Even worse was wondering how much of it the Natives knew how to operate. *At least there are no Cardassians or Drek'la around,* she thought with relief; they would almost certainly figure out something quite nasty to do with the stuff.

The away team headed into the village, still spotting no one. "Big clump of Natives about two hundred meters that direction," said Dax, pointing; she held up her hand, and everyone came to a halt upwind of the mob. "The Natives are having an intense discussion."

"Must be some kind of a town meeting," guessed the chief.

Dax scanned. "Well, everyone's over there for sure. The houses and stores are all empty."

Odo glared at Quark for several seconds. "Well?" he demanded. "I know you can hear them with those big ears you're always boasting about. What are they saying?"

Quark glared needles, but turned in the direction Dax pointed; he closed his eyes and started to mumble inaudibly.

"Out *loud,* Quark," snarled Constable Odo.

"Give me a break. There's more than one of them talking." He continued his mumble act for a solid minute, then opened his eyes. "Everybody's talking at once, and they're all saying things like 'what's she doing now,' 'did she find one yet,' 'is she getting out,' 'she doesn't have much time,' 'isn't she out of the well yet,' 'maybe she's just too young,' 'too bad, she seemed like such a bright child.' Lots of other things, but that's pretty much the consensus."

"Out of the *well*, Quark?" demanded the constable, incredulous. "With all this technology around us, you're saying they get their water from a well?"

"I don't interpret, Odo; I don't translate; I only repeat."

"Perhaps it is merely a rustic decoration," grumbled Worf. "I have seen such things in holodeck programs."

"Surely they would just turn a tap, or at least use a modern, sealed well."

"Maybe it's abandoned?" suggested Dax. She noticed that Chief O'Brien appeared anxious, looking back and forth from the group to the direction of the mob. Dax looked at him and gestured for him to spit it out.

"Pardon me, sirs, but can't we save the philosophical gobbledygook for later? There's a little girl stuck in a well over there."

Whoops. "Chief's right: double time, let's rescue a kid." *And maybe ingratiate ourselves just a wee bit with the Natives. . . .* Dax led the charge, weaving through the buildings—plastic houses and storefronts molded into asymmetrical geometric shapes made of triangles and hexagons, like pieces of a honeycomb.

She stumbled over nothing, dropping tricorder and phaser; picking them up and rubbing her shin, Dax stared back at the faint, shimmering beam along the ground, ankle high. "Watch out for the force beam," she warned.

O'Brien stepped carefully over the beam, following it left and right with his gaze. "You know, I think it's a bench."

"So? As you said, we have a damsel in distress."

"But Commander . . . if they can manipulate force beams like that, why can't they use them to levitate the little girl out of the well? For God's sake, even *we* can't make a park bench out of a mobile force beam."

Shrugging, Dax continued threading the houses toward the congregation. *But he does raise an interesting science question,* she conceded.

When they reached the last building facing on a large clearing, she finally saw the Natives. Humanoid, fortunately, and not too different from the Alpha Quadrant norm. The shape of their noses was remarkably Bajoran, enought to make Dax wonder if the ancient Bajorans, who used a type of solar sail to ply the starwinds, might be related to these natives in some way. Dax held up a hand, halting the away team at the edge of the clearing.

At Dax's command, Odo, the least vulnerable

officer, led the away team forward, followed closely by Worf, then Dax and O'Brien, with the gnomish Quark hiding in the back. As they crossed the clearing toward the mob of nearly seventy people, the murmurs from the crowd gradually faded to silence and everyone turned to look at the newcomers.

"Greetings," said Odo, making no gestures; the universal translator would turn his words into the Natives' speech, but there was no telling what a raised hand might mean on this planet. "We come from . . . another village a few days' journey from here."

"Another village?" said a gamine, nearly androgynous woman; the others deferred to her as if she were the local hetman. She looked the away team up and down. "Are you sure you don't come from another planet?"

"A-another planet?" said Dax, surprised.

"Those who occupy the cities came from another planet, so I figured you might've. You look strange enough, especially the short one with the cooling flaps."

"Cooling flaps!" shouted Quark, enraged.

"Shh," soothed Jadzia. "Quiet, Quark, or you'll never close the deal. My name is, ah, Dax. Whom have I the honor of addressing?"

"I am Asta-ha. I speak for these Tiffnaks."

Just then, a shrill burst of profanity emerged from the center of the mob, complete with reverb and echo effect. If it was the child, she seemed to be in reasonably good health; *kid has breath enough for some powerful screaming, in any event.* "Asta-ha, it sounds as if there's a little girl trapped in that well there. Do you need help getting her out?"

Asta-ha's face brightened at the suggestion. "Can you find the tool? We can't help her, of course, the poor child."

"May we take a look?" Dax dodged her way up to the lip of the well and peered over; the sun was in later afternoon, and the slanty rays didn't quite reach all the way down to where the little girl waited, presumably stuck. Still, the well walls had a high enough albedo that Dax could just pick her out in the dim, reflected sunlight. "Hold on, little girl; we'll find something to haul you up."

Jadzia Dax was answered by another long chaw from the profanity plug, which the universal translator thankfully failed to translate; the meaning was nevertheless as clear as an unstressed dilithium crystal, connecting the little girl's desire to be about ten meters higher than she was with her annoyance that she had no means to levitate herself.

O'Brien pushed his way through the crowd to join Dax at the well. "Ah, anybody have a rope?" he asked hopefully.

"And some wood," added the Trill, thinking of a painter's chair. "A chunk at least this wide and this thick."

The crowd oohed and ahhed in amazement. Asta-ha clutched at Dax's elbow. "You can raise her with such simple tech? How?"

The lieutenant commander stared for a moment, nonplussed. She opened her mouth to say something, then decided it would be unkind. *Poor woman probably got stuck with a bad set of chromosomes.* "Well, get us the rope and the wood, and we'll show you."

CHAPTER 5

FINDING A SIMPLE ROPE and hunk of wood proved harder than Miles O'Brien had anticipated. *You'd think they'd have a hardware store back in the village,* he complained silently. *Or even just a clothesline.* But at last, a couple of nameless Natives—*what did they call themselves? Tiffnaks?*—returned with the implements.

Commanders Dax and Worf busied themselves hacking the wood down to manageable size (using hands and feet, not phasers), while the chief uncoiled the rope and began tying loops for the little girl's legs to fit through; it wouldn't do to haul her halfway up, then have her tumble off the seat back down the well. The shrieks from the child lent him a sense of urgency. . . . He could just imagine that was Molly down there.

"Sir, I've got the rope ready," he cried. Dax handed him the wooden seat, and O'Brien set about carefully tying the rope to it so the loops would dangle on either side. All the while, the crowd pressed closer and closer, seemingly astonished anew by each phase of the operation; they pointed at the rope, the seat, and the knots and whispered amazed explanations to their neighbors. *I can't believe they've never even heard of a rope rescue,* thought the chief, even more amazed at the crowd's amazement. Everything he was doing was just plain common sense.

At last, they had a workable "painter's chair," on which artisans used to sit so they could decorate the sides of buildings, back in the ancient days before antigravs or even scaffolding. Worf dangled it over the mouth of the well and began to lower it, while O'Brien shone his hand torch down the shaft; curiously, the same crowd that had stood astonished at the painter's chair took the flashlight without a second glance, as if they'd seen hundreds of them, trading a score for a strip of latinum. Worf lowered the chair, swiftly but well controlled.

After a moment's silence, there was a loud thump, followed by a renewed string of cries from the innocent child. "I think we made contact," said the chief.

"Sit on the chair, honey," he shouted down the shaft. The child seemed as utterly confused as the crowd was amazed. "Little girl, sit on the chair, and we'll haul you up here." At the words "up here," the little girl's brownish face brightened into a smile. She tugged the chair down into the ankle-deep water at the bottom of the well and obediently straddled it.

The pose was all wrong; they wouldn't have made it even a meter without losing her over the side. "No no, honey; not that way. . . . Just like it was a swing."

"Swing?" she queried—the first words that the universal translator had deigned to translate.

"You know, like the swings on your playground." Blank stare. "Um . . . well, put both legs on the same side of the wooden seat—yes, now the other leg, my wee tiny colleen. That's good, honey. What's your name? Can you stick your legs through those two dangly loops, dear?"

"I'm Tivva-ma, and I'm seven."

"That's wonderful, my heart. Now Tivva-ma, can you put your legs through the little loops?"

After several minutes of begging and pleading, O'Brien, with Commander Dax's help, managed to talk Tivva-ma into the proper way to seat herself on a painter's chair. As she held on tightly, Worf pulled up the rope hand over hand; within a few seconds, Tivva-ma's dark face and bluish yellow hair appeared over the well. O'Brien made a diving catch, grabbing the girl in a strong bear hug and depositing her on dry land.

"You made it, honey. You're safe." Then he held

her back at arm's length, inspecting her with great concern. "Are you all right, Tivva-ma? Is your mommy here?"

"Yes, of course," said Asta-ha, "I haven't left."

The entire away team stared at the plump woman. *"You're* Tivva-ma's mother?" demanded an incredulous Dax.

Asta-ha seemed oblivious to the tone of shame in the commander's voice. "Why yes; she's the crown mayor, my heir."

"Does this count, Madam Mayor?" asked Tivva-ma in great trepidation.

"It was rather an unorthodox solution," mused Mayor Asta-ha, "but I *suppose* you could call this ingenious rope thing new tech of a sort." The lady mayor looked around the crowd. "Anyone want to dispute the mark?"

There was a low rumble of voices as everyone glanced back and forth at his neighbor; the hubbub gradually turned into a chorus of negative responses. "Yes, precious one," said Asta-ha, leaning hands on knees, "it counts. Congratulations on attaining the first mark."

Tivva-ma whooped and began to march around the clearing like a band leader; O'Brien stared back and forth in confusion and mounting anger. "Do you mean tae tell me," he shouted furiously, "that this whole thing was a *coming-of-age* ritual? Throwing a little girl down a well, your *own daughter?"*

Again, Asta-ha blinked in confusion. "We didn't

62

throw her down the well. What do you take us for—monsters from another planet? We lowered her quite carefully."

Something was wrong; something smelled fishy to the chief. He wrinkled his nose, savoring the taste of the lady mayor's last remark. "Wait . . . you lowered her? But—you were all shaken by the rope rescue we just did. . . . You'd never seen such a thing before. I don't understand."

"Truly, we haven't. I never realized you could do such complicated tricks with such a simple piece of new tech."

Commander Dax butted her way back into the dialogue. "Then if you don't mind us prying, Madam Mayor, how *did* you lower her down?"

Asta-ha answered slowly, as if fearing it was a trick question. "With old tech, of course. Like this. . . ."

The mayor fished a tiny piece of equipment out of her sporran; it looked like one of Dr. Bashir's hyposprays; she pointed it at Worf and depressed a button.

As Asta-ha raised the tool, the gigantic Klingon floated into the air; he began to bellow and thrash his limbs. *"Put me down. At once!"* The lady mayor held Worf dangling over their heads for a few moments, then carefully lowered him back to the ground, landing him with a gentle thump. The Klingon didn't actually attack Asta-ha, but O'Brien could tell it was only by the most extraordinary forbearance on his friend's part. If steam could erupt from a Klingon's ears, Worf would have resembled a teakettle just then.

Smoothly interceding before Worf could explode, Commander Dax said, "We would absolutely love to see your village, if you have no objection?"

"Objection? Tiffnak is open to all, unlike the angry villages across the big water."

"Can someone show us around?" persisted the Trill.

"I shall do it myself," said the mayor proudly. "Tivva-ma, the crown mayor, must be paraded through the streets anyway for her great success."

HER great success? snorted the chief to himself. "Excuse me," he interjected, "but did you say the *town* is called Tiffnak?"

"Yes. Isn't it a wonderful name?"

"What does it mean?" inquired Odo, looking around curiously at the mix of high-tech buildings and force beams and low-tech, rustic touches like the wishing well.

"It doesn't mean anything," said Asta-ha. "I thought it perfectly expressed our emotion this less-moon. As a people."

O'Brien was trying to get at something. "So when you say you people are the Tiffnaks, Mayor Asta-ha, you mean you people here in *this* town, this—ah, less-moon?"

"Don't you like the name?" asked the mayor, blinking her blue green speckled eyes at the chief;

he was almost overpowered by the urge to reach out and pat her head.

"It's a lovely name," said Dax, smiling. "But I think what O'Brien is asking is whether you will still be the Tiffnaks in, say, another couple of less-moons . . . or what people a day's journey from here would be called."

"Two less-moons? Oh, I'm sure the mood will have changed by then. We'll have lots more new tech, since we have nine ceremonies of various sorts scheduled before then. Our mood always changes with each new tech; in fact, after seeing what you gave us with rope and wood, I'd have to say that maybe Tiffnaki would be better now." Asta-ha brightened, and her nose ridges paled. "That's it! We shall have another meeting, and I'll suggest Tiffnaki. I'm sure it'll be approved."

O'Brien mulled this answer. He edged closer to the commander and spoke quietly; Asta-ha made no effort not to listen. . . . Evidently, the Tiffnaks or Tiffnakis had little concern for other people's privacy. "Commander, I'm starting to get the impression that these people *didn't* create all this technology—the force beams and such."

"They use it," she pointed out.

"I think they *find* it, but maybe they don't build it."

Dax stared at the chief, lowering her dark brows. Her spots were pale, always a bad sign.

O'Brien tried again: "What I mean is, I think

somebody else built all this stuff, and these people—Tiffnaks, or whatever they call themselves—use what they find. I think they have coming-of-age rituals where they put someone in a weird predicament, like down a well, and see if she can find some piece of 'new tech' that gets her out."

Dax whipped up her tricorder and scanned all around her, not only at the Tiffnakis but the plants surrounding them. "Well," she said, "their DNA is obviously related to that of every other living thing within tricorder range. I think they did evolve here, Chief."

Now that he listened, Chief O'Brien heard clickings and rustlings in the wide-bladed, grasslike flora at his feet; stooping low for a moment, he saw large four-legged "insects" with bodies three or four centimeters long and a pair of leg tufts at each end; he saw what looked like a worm; and in a fenced-in area near one building, he saw a furry, finned animal that looked like a cross between a wolverine and a Bajoran whipbeast sunning itself. While he watched, the animal rolled on its back and writhed, just like a dog scratching its back against the lawn. *What a cozy, domestic scene,* he thought, almost enviously.

He leaned even closer to the commander. "Well . . . maybe their ancestors invented the stuff, and somehow their civilization has degenerated? How old are these buildings?"

Dax scanned again, looked puzzled, and recalibrated. She repeated the scan. "Well, according to the decay rate of trace radioactive elements, I'd guess these buildings are at least two million years old."

"Two *million?* Are you sure, ma'am?"

Dax raised one eyebrow in a look she must have learned from some Vulcan she knew in a previous life. "I'm sure; I checked for carbon 14 in the wooden squares encased inside the plastic, but it was entirely gone. That was my first clue; I had to switch to elements with a longer half-life to get a preliminary estimate. . . . It's between two and seven million years, which makes these structures among the oldest still standing in the Alpha Quadrant."

Well, ask a stupid question. O'Brien accepted his lumps for having questioned the science officer's science. "Well, that fits in with the thesis, doesn't it, Commander? I mean, if they still had the technological know-how, they'd have torn down these old houses, or at least built new ones."

"There's not a building here that was built within the past two thousand millennia," said the commander. "They're not just using old wood chips, if that's what you're thinking, because if they were *that* old, they'd have long since rotted away— unless they were enclosed in the plastic, which I presume happened only during construction."

O'Brien blinked, wondering whether he was going to be tested. "All right, all right; I believe you, Commander."

Mayor Asta-ha (and her daughter, the crown

mayor) took them on a Cook's tour of the village; it looked pretty much like any other village on any planet in the Federation, except for the extraordinary level of technology. . . . And the trivial uses to which the Tiffnakis put it: they used antientropic heat generators to dry themselves after bathing; they used transporter technology to beam replicated groceries from one end of the town to the other; the children played on force-beam jungle gyms.

Worf sidled up to the chief while the hereditary mayor explained the use of a self-mobile tractor beam to sweep up rubbish after a picnic. "This is like the Federation gone mad," he complained bitterly. "If we are not careful, this is where we shall end up."

The tour was broken by a celebratory luncheon that was actually for Tivva-ma, having passed her first ceremony; but the Tiffnakis turned it into a welcoming for the newcomers "from another planet" as well. Tivva-ma was not exactly thrilled at sharing *her* day; but she was only the crown mayor, not the mayor.

Luncheon was somewhat a misnomer; because of the high cyanogen content of the food, which broke down into cyanide, among other chemicals poisonous to Federation and Ferengi personnel, the entire away team had to beg off the local delicacies. The chief was uncertain how to do so, but Dax explained the rudeness by resorting to the religion dodge: they were on a special diet ordained "by the tech" and could only eat the food they brought with them. Odo simply claimed not to be hungry.

Most of the food looked like exotically prepared fungus, and Chief O'Brien felt a great sense of relief that he could eat none of it; Dax, however, being more culinarily adventurous, seemed disappointed. When the Tiffnakis had bloated themselves on a magnificent fungal feast (and the away team had shoveled down some miserable combat rations, "com-rats"), the postprandial interrogation commenced.

"Mayor Asta-ha," asked Commander Dax pleasantly at luncheon, after Tavvi-ma had given a "commencement" speech that O'Brien found simultaneously charming and frightening, "you spoke of the Cardassians and Drek'la earlier. How do you know about them?"

"Oh, it's all across the bush," said the mayor. "They have overwhelmed several villages not far from here. They live in the abandoned centers and strike outward, trying to conquer all the different people, I suppose."

"Ah, gravy please," said the chief, pointing at the away team gravy boat being monopolized by Quark. "Thank you, your . . . mayorship. Doesn't that concern you, aliens having conquered and destroyed whole villages?" demanded O'Brien, incredulous that she could be so blasé about the obliteration of her own people.

"Yes, it might pose some risk to the Tiffnakis, but we have a great deal of new tech, surely much more than did the worthless and unsuccessful villages that fell to the invaders. You're sure you wouldn't like some succulent fungus?"

"No . . . no thank you." Chief O'Brien stared around the table, seeing only mirrors of Asta-ha's own mask of unconcern. Sensor readings now indicated Cardassian life signs within seventy klicks, but nobody appeared to care. "Look," he added, "maybe you're not aware of what some aliens can do to the people they conquer. Odo? Explain, will you?"

"Yes," admitted the constable reluctantly, "I'm afraid I do know a bit about it." He proceeded to regale the mayor and her contingent for several minutes on the atrocities visited upon the Bajorans by their Cardassian masters, the scars still left behind.

"But that's terrible," cried Asta-ha, her mouth dropping open.

The mayor shook her head, clucking in sympathy. But still, she didn't seem to connect the stories and the pillaging of the other villages with imminent danger to her own townful of Tiffnakis.

"If you don't mind my asking," tried O'Brien, starting to feel frustrated, "how did the other villages fall? I mean, you have enough tech here, new and old, even just what little bit I can figure out, to send the Cardassians packing. How could the other Natives—the other villages lose?"

Asta-ha took on a dreamy aspect. "They must

not have found favor in
opined. Looking heavenward,
naks—I mean Tiffnakis—are belo
the tech."

"Um, how do you know?"

Blinking her way back to the here and no   ie
mayor said, "Isn't it obvious? Were we not so
favored, would this marvelous and exciting new
tech have been given us? Imagine, a rope and a
stick that has the power of an antigrav." She looked
so excited that O'Brien hadn't the heart to continue the inquisition.

Later, after luncheon and after the away team
had been shown every point of interest in the
town—no churches or temples, O'Brien noticed,
not even one to "the tech"; replicators but no fields
or stockyards; technology for entertainment put
upon the same level of importance as that for
survival—the team huddled to voice their observa-
tions. At first, Asta-ha stood right next to them,
listening in a polite but somewhat uninterested
fashion, until Commander Dax asked if she could
leave; the mayor toddled off without apparently
taking offense.

"All right, people," said the commander, "I want
to pull everything together before we contact the
ship; I want to give the captain answers, not
questions."

"Frankly," said the chief, kicking off the discussion (which he considered his right whenever the

…as engineering and technology), "I don't think they have anything to worry about. I don't know the half of how these weapons work"—he gestured at a haphazard pile of devices that the Tiffnakis said they used to defend against other villages' tech-raiding parties—"I mean, they might be excavation tools, for all I know. But they make damned good weapons; I saw Asta-ha's little daughter Tivva-ma, no older than Molly, carve a furrow in a hillside with that thing over there that looks like a magic wand."

"I concur with the chief," said Worf, his deep *basso* vibrating O'Brien's teeth in their sockets. "There is much here that Starfleet should investigate."

"Such as, besides the earth-moving equipment?" Dax seemed considerably brighter at the news that they had good stock to work with in defending the planet from the Cardassians.

"There is a personalized force shield that somewhat resembles those used by the Borg," said Worf.

"And a projection device that I'd swear can drain power from a phaser or disruptor at a distance," added O'Brien, remembering a fast demonstration by one of the other Tiffnakis, a tall man with one blue-speckled eye and one red-speckled. "I couldn't actually try it out because I wasn't sure whether we should allow them to see our phasers."

Quark spoke up. "By the Divine Treasury, do you people even realize what we're *sitting on* here? This is the greatest technological treasure trove since—since I found the wormhole. . . . Or even since the first Grand Nagus invented warp drive."

"Ah," sneered Odo, "the new toys have driven all thoughts of strip-mining the landscape out of the tiny lump of latinum that stands in for Quark's brain."

The Ferengi glared at his old nemesis; not for the first time, O'Brien found it somewhat surreal that the animosity/friendship between the constable and the Ferengi smuggler went back *much* farther than the discovery of the wormhole (by Captain Sisko, not by Quark), or the liberation of Bajor. . . . In fact, the pair had known and hated each other with passion since long before the Federation even knew of the existence of *Deep Space Nine,* then called *Terek Nor.* The marriage of hatred between Quark and Odo predated O'Brien's marriage of love with Keiko, which seemed to have been around forever. Sisko was probably still a lieutenant commander without even his own ship yet when Quark and Odo met and discovered revulsion at first sight, and Major Kira was probably rankless and hiding in a cave. With a connection of hatred going back so far into the mists of antiquity, how could Quark and Odo *not* be the closest of enemies?

"Constable Odo," said the Ferengi, with a deep undertone of "talking to the idiot child" rippling behind his words, "any fool would realize that brand-new technology, especially weapons in time of war, would be far more lucrative than mere minerals. Any fool would jump at the chance to profiteer—I mean profit—from such a discovery."

"Yes, Quark," said the constable, smirking slightly, "any *fool.*"

"Time's up," chirped Dax. "That was your one exchange for the day. Now let's get back to business. . . . Quark, your zeal to exploit the resources and technology of these people is duly noted; it will be greatly to your credit when you reach the Divine Treasury."

"Well, all right then," he mumbled, but continued working his mouth—*as if trying to weigh the whole planet on a latinum scale,* the chief thought.

O'Brien took a deep breath and broached the subject that had started nagging at him while they discussed what they had seen. "Commander, I'm a bit concerned about the Prime Directive. . . . How do we apply it in this case?"

Worf had an opinion on that subject, too. "Surely it does not apply to cultures this technologically advanced."

"But these people are not spacefarers," protested the chief. "They only barely know they live on a planet. They don't even have a one-world government. . . . How could they be considered an advanced civilization?"

"They use warp technology," insisted the Klingon, gesturing angrily at the pile of stuff on the table. "Several of these devices are offshoots of warp technology, including the power-draining device and the personal shields. Chief O'Brien will confirm my observation."

"Well, *technically* that's true," admitted the chief; he was reluctant to interject his position in between that of two lieutenant commanders and a security chief, which must be a rank at least equal to full, three-pip commander.

"The planet's already been invaded, so any violations have already been committed; the Natives are already fighting—and we want to keep our presence here secret in any event," said Dax.

O'Brien, satisfied that the officers had arrived at a consensus that he, the lone enlisted man, could definitely live with, tried to steer the meeting to a close so he could get back to something important: playing with the new toys to see what he could learn. "I think we can report to the captain that the Natives are mobilizing against the Drek'la and the spoon-heads—I'm sorry, been hanging around the major too long—the Cardassians."

Worf suddenly sniffed the air; he looked around, wetting his finger and raising it as high as he could. He looked like a man who had a strong suspicion about something.

Plucking Commander Dax's tricorder from her belt, he poked at it and then made a sweep. When Worf realized everyone was staring at him, he cleared his throat. "Well, we are about to find out whether the chief's observation about the—the planetary natives is accurate."

"Why, Commander?" asked O'Brien, already feeling the familiar tightening in his belly and urgent desire to find a handy tree that he always felt just before combat.

Dax looked over Worf's shoulder down at the tricorder. "Because we're about to have extraplanetary visitors," she said; "the Drek'la are coming. . . . They're about forty kilometers distant and moving fast."

CHAPTER
6

ASTA-HA CAME scurrying up to the away team, proving that the Tiffnakis, at least, had as good an early-warning system as did the Federation. "Enemies coming, like you were talking about. Can you fight?"

"We can fight," said Worf; then remembering what Jadzia had ordered, he added, "You must arm us."

"Spoken no faster than undertaken," said a short man at Worf's elbow; his blue-and-red hair crest was elaborately curled alternating left and right, grooming that doubtless took hours to perfect. The man handed Worf a tiny toy that looked and felt like a finger torch, a child's flashlight operated by squeezing the plastic sides together. Worf scowled down at it, wondering whether he was being made light of. . . . But he had enough respect for the technology of the Natives not to point it at anyone he liked.

O'Brien was handed a man-sized rifle with sights and a trigger, adding to the humiliation; the Klingon almost offered to trade with the chief, but he reflected that it would be dishonorable.

Jadzia received the excavating tool that Chief O'Brien referred to as a "faerie wand," while Quark and Odo were each given tubes with tiny bumps. "Um . . . um . . . what do I do with this?" demanded the panicky Ferengi.

"I don't know every function yet," said Hair Crest, "but I've discovered that if you point this end at the enemy and press this yellow nodule, his skin cracks, causing intense pain."

"But—but what do the blue-and-gray nodules do?" demanded Quark, staring in horror at the innocuous-looking tube. Hair Crest shrugged, unconcerned, and the Ferengi staggered away muttering curses befitting his cowardly shopkeeper's personality.

Constable Odo seemed quite happy with his tube. Worf edged close enough that no one would overhear. "Perhaps you should shapeshift into one of the planetary natives, to further confuse the Cardassians. We do not want to be discovered."

"I think it might upset the Natives, as you call

them, if they saw me changing shape before their eyes . . . don't you think?"

Worf frowned; much as he tried to avoid it, the psychology of the individual kept cropping up. "A warrior does not concern himself with such fears," he muttered, retreating to the front line.

Such as it was . . . there was no military organization, not even any attempt on the part of the Natives to find cover or concealment. Jadzia and the rest of the away team had found outlying buildings to hide behind, and Worf joined them, but the mayor, Asta-ha, and the other Natives simply stood in a clump, monkeying with their weapons and waiting for the Cardassians to slaughter them.

"What are they *doing?*" urgently demanded the Klingon in Jadzia's ear.

"Best guess? To them, technology *is* warfare. They don't have any idea what to do but stand in the middle of the road and fire their tech at anything unfriendly that approaches."

"Have they never fought in any wars?"

Jadzia shrugged. "Why don't you ask them? Maybe you can get them to hide behind something, at least."

"How long until contact?"

"The advance has stopped. It looks like our friends are waiting for something. Interesting. I'm showing a force of Drek'la led by a solitary Cardassian."

"Perhaps the Cardassians allied with the Drek'la when their ships were captured." Worf rose, snuck a quick peek in the direction where the Cardassian invaders waited, then trotted to Asta-ha. He was shocked to see that she had her daughter Tivva-ma with her . . . and the young girl also carried a weapon.

Is this the honor of a young warrior? he wondered, *or is it complete ignorance of the danger?* "Mayor Asta-ha . . . have your people, the, ah, Tiffnakis, ever fought a war before?"

"War?" She pronounced the word as if it had not been translated by the universal translator . . . perhaps because the natives had no word for war in their language.

"Do you have—enemies?"

Asta-ha's puzzled look turned to sudden understanding. "Oh, enemies all around! There are the Dav who live over the hill toward the needle; we aren't very friendly with the Tiffnakis, either."

Now it was Worf's turn to be puzzled. "But . . . *you* are the Tiffnakis."

"Yes. Do you like the name?"

"How can you be on unfriendly terms with the Tiffnakis if—"

"What? No, *we're* the Tiffnakis; it's the Tiffnakis we have to worry about. They live to the left hand of the needle."

Worf snorted loudly; clearly, there was a nuance of pronunciation that he could not hear. "Very well. But should you not get to cover to more effectively kill your enemies?"

Asta-ha looked blank. "Cover?"

"It is—you use . . ." Worf had what O'Brien would call a "brainstorm." "It is another piece of our new tech: you use the buildings as a . . . new-tech shield against disruptors. As we are doing, see?"

The female's astonishment was painful for Worf to see. Clearly, no such thing had ever occurred to her in all her life; it was, truly, new "technology" to her—the simplest, most rudimentary of tactics. Without bothering to thank the Klingon—why not? did not "new tech" fall from the trees every day? —she bustled to her comrades to demonstrate the gift from the tech.

Satisfied for the moment, Worf returned to the away team, still feeling a vague disquiet. "There is something very wrong with these people," he complained.

"Well, we're about to see whether it affects their ability to defend themselves."

"Our friends are moving."

"They paused for five minutes, then started to roll again." Dax stood, called loud enough for her own troops to hear: "Stand ready, men."

Worf crouched, holding his weapon at arm's length to get a better sight picture; he felt the thrill of battle surge though him. . . . *I am alive, a Klingon, a WARRIOR!* He could barely contain his glee when he saw the dust kicked up from the Cardassian skimmers darken the eastern horizon—"the right hand of the needle," the natives would probably say, assuming their needles pointed to magnetic north.

Worf held his fire until the first blast came from the enemy. Then he squeezed his flashlight. Nothing. . . . He tried again and again, but the weapon was dead.

"Blast," he snarled. "Somebody give me a weapon; mine has malfunctioned."

In front of the Klingon, Jadzia threw her "faerie wand" to the ground in disgust and drew her phaser, but Worf swiftly grabbed her hand and pointed the weapon towards the dirt. "No, Jadzia. We must not let them know Starfleet is here."

Snarling like a true Klingon woman (to Worf's marveling eyes), Jadzia stood and spoke in command tones: "Does anyone have a working Tiffnaki weapon?"

From O'Brien's passionate, rich, Irish cursing, Quark's temper tantrum, and Odo's look of disgust, Worf understood the answer even without anyone answering. Running across the gap to the natives, who now milled about in total shock and confusion, he discovered that their weapons, too, had simply ceased working. There was not a man or woman in the entire village whose tech would operate. . . . Somehow, the Cardassians had turned it all off.

Jadzia leapt up and gave the hardest order for any warrior to give: "Retreat!" she shouted, waving to the Natives; they stared in confusion—evidently, it was yet another piece of "new tech" they had never seen. "Run away," she tried, to no avail. "Are you deaf?" she shouted, pointed rearwards. "Point yourselves in that direction and *run like the wind!*"

A few of the natives understood, including Astaha and the mayor's daughter; they turned and ran, slowly at first, then in panic as the Drek'la leisurely opened fire with their disruptors on the clumped group. Worf caught a glimpse of Natives being torn to shreds by the Cardassian weapons, then he, too, was forced into the ignominy of running away like a *dubhop* being chased by a hunter.

It was easy to escape; the Drek'la were in no hurry. The away team and approximately two hundred of the Tiffnakis kept running until they had put five kilometers between themselves and the village; the Drek'la stopped in the settlement and settled in, at least for the night. The first pitched battle between the Drek'la and the Federation for the tiny mud ball Sierra-Bravo 112-II was a rout.

Worf grabbed Jadzia by the arm as she limped past, trailing blood. She refused to rest until after she made sure O'Brien, Quark, and Odo were safely stowed, as a Klingon would. Her eyes were the color of violets with flames around their edges, or the Klingon Sea of the Stand when the sun was nearly set in the distant waters. Her face burned with shame, and the Trill spots were dark against her bone white skin. She looked like the goddess of death.

"It was not your fault," Worf said, offering a warrior's comfort. "It was a system failure that you could not anticipate."

Major Kira sat in Ops, sipping tea and musing on the wild workings of chance and fate. She closed her eyes and listened to the hum of the station. . . . What had been *Deep Space Nine* was now *Emissary's Sanctuary*—and it was running like a Bajoran children's prayer top.

To Kira's immense frustration and annoyance beyond her (political) ability to say, every senseless move Kai Winn had made had turned out perfectly: the vedeks and flatterers she had placed in charge of every aspect of station operations, tossing out men and women who had done their jobs with *éclat* for years, turned out, each and every one, to be brilliant bureaucrats; and contrary to everything the major had always believed, good bureaucrats were exactly what the station truly needed all this time.

The vedeks managed to bring out the best and most selfless devotion in the workers, and jobs that were done only haphazardly at best under Captain Sisko sparkled under Governor Kai Winn. The infrastructure of the station, which Miles had spent every waking hour complaining about, was systematically replaced with fine Bajoran craftsmanship; it could have been done under the Federation, but it would have taken every hand working triple-overtime shifts around the clock for a week . . . which was exactly what the new Bajoran workers did at a word from the Kai.

Devotions at the temple had never been better attended; even the replicators seemed to work better; the food tasted like the devices were being overhauled every other day—*which they probably are,* thought Kira in mingled awe and bitterness.

At this rate, far from replacing the Kai as governor of the station, Shakar would be lucky to keep his post as First Minister. "Oh, Prophets," breathed Kira, eyes still tightly shut and head back, "if only she could face a small crisis or two. Just a little one—it's all I ask."

Immediately, Kira felt a chill run along her spine. "Be careful what you wish, for you may get it" was as common a saying on Bajor as it was in the Federation. She had the most terrible feeling that such prayers, especially this close to the wormhole, the lair of the Prophets, were far too easily heard: something was surely about to go terribly wrong.

CHAPTER
7

THE FIRST disruptor blast took Major Kira completely by surprise. There'd been no warning.

There they were, eleven ships, to be precise. They'd plowed out of the wormhole in minutes. Not one of them showed up on *Deep Space Nine's* deep-imaging sensors, none tripped the early-warning alerts. There was nothing.

When the pounding began, the first thing Kira did was raise the shields; while they were still rising in intensity, she scanned for enemies. At last, she switched to straight visible-light viewing—"looking out the window," as O'Brien called it—and that was when she finally saw the eleven ships. According to the scanners, they weren't even present.

"Dominion," said Kira to no one, since the last time she checked, she was alone on the Ops floor; Kai Winn's patronage appointees still refused to show up for their watches, though she had to admit they had done a good job with the routine aspects of running *Deep Space Nine*. . . . *No, it's* Emissary's Sanctuary *now,* she thought, smiling at the grim joke. Some sanctuary.

"Are you sure, child?" said Kai Winn from directly behind the major. Kira jumped and spun around. How could such an out-of-shape woman as the Kai move so quickly and quietly, on a station that was heaving with every hammer blow?

"Kai! Sure about what?"

"That it's the Dominion."

Kira returned to her threat board. "I can't aim the damned phasers. . . . The sensors don't even see them." Kira tried a couple of line-of-sight shots, but the attackers were moving too quickly, making random evasive turns. "Who else would it be? They came through the wormhole, and they don't show up on the sensor array." But she didn't even recognize the ship design—they were like no Dominion ships she had ever seen.

The Kai seemed remarkably cool, enough so that Kira noticed in the heat of battle. "Isn't there any other weapon you can bring to bear against them?" she asked.

"Yes, of course. The quantum torpedos—they don't have to be precise hits." Kira snapped the guards off the arming touchplates and proceeded to arm the thousand torpedoes that Captain Sisko had installed against just such an eventuality. Her hands were working so quickly, she had already moved to key in the launch sequence before realizing that the board had not caught up with her.

PLEASE ENTER AUTHORIZATION PASSWORD:

Kira blinked, staring at the message. The computer's mellifluous voice repeated it out loud.

"Child, what are you waiting for?" asked the Kai, leaning over Kira's shoulder. "Enter the password."

"There is no password," blurted Major Kira, shocked.

"But Kira, it *asks* for one."

"It never has before." Kira half rose, forcing Kai Winn to stand quickly to avoid contact. "Damn it! Ah . . . ah—Kira Nerys, authorization Bravo-Alpha-Bravo-Echo. . . . Unlock the damned torpedoes!"

"I'm sorry," said the computer with detached efficiency, "but that is not an authorization password. Please enter authorization password."

There it was, staring her in the face. . . .

PLEASE ENTER AUTHORIZATION PASSWORD:

"Blood of the Prophets!"

"Child?"

"Sorry—um, Sisko, Benjamin, authorization . . ." She struggled to remember what she once had overheard the captain say to unlock a personal message from Starfleet Command; she had never used the code herself, of course, and it took her a second to remember . . . a second during which the attackers fired two more salvos, jerking the station noticeably, even right through the shields. "Authorization Hugo-Uniform-November-Kilo."

"I'm sorry, but that is not an authorization password. Please enter authorization password."

Kira felt a flush of horrified understanding creep up her neck and across her face. She hadn't expected the code to work, since the computer would realize she was not Captain Sisko, but it gave *the wrong error message.* She had expected the computer to respond, "Invalid use of authorization password," which would mean she had to tear into the circuits and cross her voice patterns in the main database clip with those of the captain. But the response had been the same as to her own normal authorization code.

Kira turned and discovered to her astonishment that the Kai had vanished; but a moment later, the turbolift arrived carrying six mean-looking Bajorans, four men and two women; they hustled to the Ops battle stations without sparing a glance at Kira: two at Dax's console, one at Worf's, and the other two with heavy phaser rifles scanning the room with low-intensity phaser beams to flush out any changelings who might have infiltrated as seat cushions or pieces of equipment.

The Kai reappeared on Sisko's balcony. "My flock, the *Emissary's Sanctuary* is under attack by unknown enemies from the Gamma Quadrant; they may be Dominion or may not . . . but we must defend ourselves and our planet, regardless."

The combat team looked at the Kai with such reverence that Kira felt outnumbered and uncomfortable. Then they turned their attention to the phasers.

She had no complaints about their competence; they were a professional phaser crew either from a Bajoran patrol ship or from the planetary defense forces themselves. "Sensors out—visual track, follow my tracer. . . . One-mark, two-mark, three-mark—pattern analysis. . . . Are they repeating?—bracketing shots . . . clipped one, no telemetry.

Kira found herself excluded from the fight. Nobody told her to leave, but she quickly lost track of what the combat crew were saying—they spoke in the code word staccato of a squad that had lived, eaten, slept, trained, and fought together for months or years. Realizing that she was about as necessary as a piloting stick on a runabout, Kira stood down from her console and joined the Kai on the balcony.

Kai Winn followed the battle with hard, calculating eyes; she betrayed no emotions and even offered intelligent and workable suggestions to the team (which accepted them gratefully). "They're trying to get close enough to launch boarding parties," warned one of the two women at Dax's console.

"Seal the station," ordered the Kai.

"Kai Winn," said Kira in great urgency, "I have to contact the Federation and get the authorization codes for those torpedoes."

Without looking away from Ops, which had become a de facto CIC, a combat information center, the Kai responded forcefully: "I'm sorry, child, I absolutely forbid it."

"But without the torpedoes, we'll never—"

"This is a test sent by the Prophets, Major; we must survive without the help of your Federation. I have already sent for Bajoran destroyers."

Kira's mouth was dry; she tried to lick her lips, but there was no moisture. The station was struck by a particularly close hit, and the deck yawed left, nearly dropping Kira over the railing to the floor below. The Kai crouched, clutching the rail tightly; the combat crew didn't react.

"Bajoran destroyers won't stand up against these disruptor blasts," warned Kira. "The most they can do is distract the ships long enough for us to get a clean shot."

"Then they will distract the enemy ships, child," said the Kai, still following the performance in Ops rather than the conversation she wasn't quite having with Major Kira.

Gritting her teeth, the major spoke in a hoarse whisper. "Kai, *the Federation will release the torpedoes*—this is an emergency. With the quantum torpedoes, we can blow these jerks to hell and back, right back through the wormhole to the Gamma

Quadrant. *Don't you understand?* We *need* those codes."

For the first time since the assault began, the Kai looked directly at Kira. "I am in command of *Emissary's Sanctuary,* child. You are my executive officer. The decision is mine to make, and I will not run to the Federation for help." She closed her eyes, tilting her head back. "We are all in the hands of the Prophets now."

Kira waited a long moment, searching her heart for what she should do, for Bajor, for Sisko, for her friends and enemies still aboard the station: for Jake, for Keiko, for Rom . . . even for that lousy excuse for a Cardassian, Garak. "Yes . . . my Kai," she said at last. Winn was right; there was no other way out for Bajor—and the future of Bajor trumped everything else.

"Hadn't you better begin organizing the defenses, Major?"

"But your combat crew is handling it perfectly well. I couldn't do any better."

Kai Winn looked directly at Kira again, and this time, the major saw in the old woman's eyes the same granite she had seen in the captain's when he stood on the same balcony, overlooking a team much like the one in the CIC below (a team that always included Major Kira). "You had better prepare the internal defenses, child; call out the station militia." Winn handed Kira a data clip. "This fight is not going to be easy or quick, I believe; I've been here before. Prepare for forcible boarding."

Kira stared at the viewers; she had a good look at the ships every time they passed one of the camera eyes while shooting and dodging return fire: she had definitely never seen the design before. "Who the hell *are* these guys?" she asked, but the Kai had already returned full attention to her CIC and the combat crew running the desperate defense of *Emissary's Sanctuary.*

Kira Nerys slid down the ladderway, feet and hands upon the rails, and darted for the turbolift platform, snatching up her personal phaser en route; she was almost thrown to the deck by a shot that set the rotational axis of the station swinging gently, like a pendulum, for several cycles before the gyros restabilized *Emissary's Sanctuary.*

Sealed by the turbolift after leaving Ops, Kira tapped her combadge and said, "Computer, scan all messages from Starfleet to *Deep Space Nine*— or, ah, *Emissary's Sanctuary*—since the turnover, in particular any verbal explanation of the message locking out the quantum torpedoes."

"There is no record of a transmission locking out the quantum torpedoes."

"Headers of all nonroutine message traffic from the Federation Council to the senior staff of the station."

The computer began rattling off a list of message headers, most having to do with administrative elements of the turnover, but then Kira heard, "Message thirty-eight of forty-four, weapon extension lockout explanatory communiqué."

"Stop. Read me that message."

Another booming pair of assaults testified to the battle still raging beyond the hull—the station was holding its own, but it couldn't continue forever. *The damned Bajoran ships better arrive soonest,* thought Kira, gritting her teeth; *the brief distraction might be the only hope we have.*

"Please enter authorization password."

Oh, Prophets. Here we go again. But when Kira gave her own code, "Kira Nerys, Bravo-Alpha-Bravo-Echo," the computer accepted it without qualm; evidently, the accompanying text was not as highly secure as the torpedoes themselves.

"The Federation Council regrets that the new administration must be informed that certain classified extensions of the weapons subsystems of the station formerly known as *Deep Space Nine* have been reallocated to a terminated state pending approval of subsequent demonstrations of successful operation of station service optimization protocols; at time of such approval, normal preoperative status of the affected subsystems will be reinitialized into a resumptive condition."

Translation, thought Kira, who really was becoming quite an expert at burospeak; *after a while, if you don't blow up the station, we'll send the signal to unlock your torpedoes.* But what was a while?

How long—a week? The Bajorans had run the station for nearly a week already, and there clearly had been no reinitialization into a resumptive condition. A month? The end of the sixty-day trial period?

With a chill, Major Kira realized they were enmeshed in a terrible struggle against unknown enemies while blind and crippled: they could neither see the attackers on the sensor array nor use the only weapon that didn't require precision aiming.

And of course, much as it galled the major to admit it, Kai Winn was right: if Bajor were to go screaming to the Federation for help now, barely a week into the turnover, the chances of it being made permanent were like unto those of finding a shrine to the Prophets on Cardassia Prime.

The old—woman—gets another point, she glumly admitted. The Kai had been full of surprises lately, from her efficiency at running the station to her startling capacity for command under fire. Add now an insightful analysis of Federation psychology. Every such success stuck in Kira's throat like a bone splinter, one more stone in the pouch of First Minister Shakar, weighing down his chances; he was already swimming upstream by trying to force the government to remain secular, when the Kai and most Bajorans clearly preferred rule by vedek decree.

The turbolift jerked to a stop at the Promenade

level, and Kira pushed into a scene from a madhouse: civilians, nearly all Bajoran, were running to and fro in a frenzy; some were injured by the shaking, though no shot had yet penetrated the shields, and with every blow, more civilians fell to the ground screaming or ran into each other or tried to rush the turbolifts that could take them to the habitat rings, the launch bays, and presumed "safety" away from the station.

The Kai's security guards refused to allow the civvies to storm the lifts, quite properly: they were needed to transport the security forces (the one area that Kai Winn had packed but not purged). "Commander," shouted Kira.

The acting CO in Odo's absence, Dag Haraia, ran to Kira and saluted; Kira was nonplussed for a moment. . . . No one ever saluted on *Deep Space Nine.* Then she remembered that he was now "militarized" and under arms, which changed things considerably. "Dag, round up these people"—she handed Dag the data clip of names she had gotten from the Kai—"and arm them; put men at every port and airlock and shoot anyone coming through; and *get these damned civilians into the shelters.*"

"Yes ma'am!" he shouted; he saluted again and ran to his lieutenants.

Kira was surprised to catch herself taking a moment to pray: *Please, O Prophets,* she said clearly in her head, *don't make me be the one to have to explain it all to the captain.* "The big one that didn't quite get away," she muttered to herself, but she was too busy to listen.

Limping from her wound, which was still bleeding slightly, Lieutenant Commander Jadzia Dax led the rest of the away team, plus Asta-ha (the hereditary mayor of the no-longer-extant village of the Tiffnakis) and the surviving members of her entourage, over a pair of hills that she named Dreary and Black, across a stream that O'Brien dubbed the Anna Liffey, and through a wood. (The trees were the same scintillant blue and green as the Natives' eyes.) They had put fifteen kilometers between themselves and the Drek'la, who camped in the ruins of the town after disruptor fire cut the two-million-year-old buildings to shards; Dax decided they were safe for the moment.

If the worst came, and the Drek'la struck too quickly for them to bug out conventionally, the Trill had already decided they would call for an emergency beam-out of everyone, and to hell with the Prime Directive. "It's too bad we can't move any faster," she said. "Are you sure none of your neighbors has any tech for moving quickly along the ground . . . say, something with wheels or floating on an antigravity field?"

Asta-ha shook her head; her daughter Tivva-ma, who announced she was still seven, shook her head at exactly the same time, causing both Dax and of course Chief O'Brien to chuckle. "Damn," muttered Dax; she wondered whether she could talk

Sisko into having the *Defiant* replicate a vehicle and beam it down where they could "stumble" across it.

"Please watch your language, Commander," cautioned the chief. "There are young ones present."

"Um, sorry about that, Chief." The Curzon within her ached to cut loose with a stream of profanity that would straighten out O'Brien's hair and turn it white, but Jadzia Dax controlled it.

Asta-ha sighed. "Yes, too bad. If you really wanted to get somewhere fast, we could use the Instantator tech in the village of the Shignavs. But I'm afraid I have no tech of the kind you seek."

"The . . . Instantator?" Dax suddenly had a horrible feeling she knew exactly what they were talking about . . . and it could have saved them a lot of grueling travel.

"I have seen it in operation," breathed the hereditary mayor. "You step into a booth, sparkles obscure your body, and you disappear—only to reappear days' and scores of days' travel distant, in the next booth." She described the obvious transporter with such holy reverence, Dax almost felt like bowing her head; from the description, Dax realized that, like the one in the Tiffnaki village for food, it was a booth-to-booth device, but sophisticated even by Federation standards. *Still,* she sighed, *it would have been useful.*

Quark came limping up to the group, moaning and trying to massage his calves while still walking;

he was followed closely by his elongated shadow, Constable Odo, sneering at every Ferengi protestation of weakness, being done for, and prediction of dire consequences.

"Oh, get off it, Quark; you're *going* to make it, because no one is going to pick you up and carry you. Honestly, you're like a spoiled child at an excessively permissive nursery school."

"Have a little heart, Odo. . . . Or better yet, why don't you make one?"

"It's too much effort to bother with unnecesary internal organs, Quark; besides, I'm happy as I am. Too bad you can't say the same about yourself."

The Ferengi sneered. "Well, you certainly didn't put any effort into a *brain,* now did you?"

"Oh, very funny. I'm hysterical, ha, ha, ha. Let's see how your quadrant-famous sense of humor gets you through your upcoming ordeal: selling your banned bar and becoming an *employee* of Kai Winn."

Quark shuddered. "I'd tell you to bite your tongue, if you had one."

"Gee . . . I wonder whether Rom has unloaded the bar to some luckless Bajoran yet?" Quark simply glared, so Odo won the round.

"Boys, boys," said Dax halfheartedly; in truth, she was barely listening to them bicker. . . . She was far more concerned about what had happened back at the village of the Tiffnakis. *I blew it. I screwed it up and nearly got everyone killed.* Now that the immediate danger was past, and they were far enough away to feel a little safety, Commander Dax began to get the shakes. The more she thought about the Cardassian raid, the more like a fiasco it looked.

"I think I've figured it out," said O'Brien, plopping down on the dewy teal grass with a disassembled mass of components in his hand; the jumble used to be a disruptor rifle. He glared at the hunk of disassembled junk—then turned a sympathetic gaze on Dax herself. She leapt to an interpretation: *even the chief thinks I completely screwed up the mission,* she raged to herself; *it's only the sheerest luck that we weren't all butchered back there.*

Dax started to realize that she could have, *should* have, evacuated the village; if she had, a hundred dead Tiffnakis, including a dozen children, would still be alive. She felt sick.

"You figured out what happened back at the defense?" she asked, leaning forward too eagerly, trying to drive deep inside thoughts of her own terrible command decisions. "What went wrong with all the weapons?"

"Nothing, Commander; nothing at all." O'Brien sounded bitter, and he looked like he wanted to spit into the mechanism.

"Nothing?"

"But it looks like it runs on some kind of *broadcast power,* of a variety our tricorders couldn't detect. The Drek'la must've somehow cut that power before attacking."

But would Asta-ha have withdrawn anyway?

"You mean, Chief, that there isn't a single backup power source anywhere around here?"

"No, Commander"—the chief scanned with his own tricorder—"I've adjusted my tricorder and can now get faint readings of the kind of power being broadcast. The nearest power source I can detect is four hundred kilometers away."

While they spoke, Worf, Quark, and Odo had joined them. "Gentlemen," said Dax, "I've got a very bad feeling about this whole mission. If all the enemy has to do is kill the lights and pull the plug, then we are in giant-sized trouble."

Worf spoke up, immediately seeing the tactical situation: "The natives will have to learn to fight on their own, even without their devices."

Dax looked at the Klingon and felt a chill; was he looking at her with a faint trace of charity? Was he? If he was, she couldn't stand that.

"Fight and *win*," corrected Dax. Her wound was painful, possibly infected, and the pain was making it hard to think. Courage and bravado can take me only so far; there's more than my pride at stake here. As much as I'd like to finish this mission, it's time, as Benjamin would say, time to call in a relief pitcher.

"People," she said, "I'm kicking this decision upstairs. And I'm taking myself out of the game."

CHAPTER 8

CAPTAIN BENJAMIN SISKO materialized in a loose wood, the trees not quite thick enough for cover or dense enough for concealment; but there were enough of them to make any disruptor shot tricky. As soon as he appeared, he glanced first at Worf, then Odo, then O'Brien; the three stood alert but not tense, and the captain relaxed a bit.

He had just completed a very unsatisfactory and alarming conversation with Dax. She had filled him in somewhat but wanted the captain to make his own assessment before she made her full report . . . so his tactical judgment wouldn't be "influenced by expectation." He had reassured her that there was little she could have done differently without psychic abilities . . . but she was still furious at herself for not foreseeing the future and preventing the deaths of the villagers.

The away team stood by themselves on a small rise; water welled from underground at the base of the rise, trickling down to form a meandering, sluggish stream that cut mostly northeast, eventually becoming a tributary to the largish river that Dax reported crossing (which the chief called the Anna Liffey, after the river that bisected old Dublin, fabled in song and legend). The rest of the escapees, two hundred and twenty of them, huddled across the ministream, fire-shocked and shaken not only by the suddenness of their loss—many of their friends, enemies, and neighbors had died, including children—but, if Dax was right, as much by the sudden loss of their tech from heaven: they had nothing, for nothing worked. They didn't even know enough to build shelters or campfires against the coming cold night.

"Fill me in," said Sisko to his away team. They did so. "All right"—Sisko looked toward the alien threat to the east—"let's hear some strategic team thinking: what are we going to do about the situation?"

This time, Worf was first to speak; he was on familiar, rehearsed ground. "We must set up an immediate military training facility," he advised, "and forge these people into an effective fighting force against the invaders."

"And what do you expect them to fight with?" demanded O'Brien. "Spears? Bows and arrows?"

"If necessary."

"But they don't even know the first thing about even *that* level of technology, Worf. They don't have any math, any physics or engineering, no materials science, nothing of chemistry or field flow, no plasma technology. . . . Nothing that could possibly discommode the enemy or even slow them up. They would roll over the Natives like—like Klingon warriors across a Boy Scout troop."

Worf growled deep in his throat, but he said nothing in response to the chief. Odo, standing unnaturally straight—like a changeling, not like a solid, who had to balance on muscles and bone—cleared his throat. "Sir, perhaps it would be better to begin at the beginning."

"Teach them basic math, engineering, and chemistry?" asked the captain skeptically.

"As Worf said, 'if necessary.'"

"Necessary it may be, Constable, but is it workable? Chief O'Brien, how long would it take you to teach a crash course in the fundamentals of weapons engineering, just concentrating on what they need to build bombs, guns, and other destructive devices?"

The chief squatted on his haunches, dipping his knees in the moist ground; he tapped away at his tricorder, presumably figuring out what he would need to teach. Then he stood, shaking his head. "It's hopeless, sir. Unless the Natives are engineering supergeniuses, it'll take months of academic work, and we don't have that much time."

"And there is more to it than that," said Worf glumly, obviously realizing he was shooting down his own idea. "It takes more than weapons to make an army, as we have just seen demonstrated. It takes organization and leadership, as well as an understanding of long-range strategy and short-term tactics."

"Aren't these Natives organized at *all?*" Sisko couldn't believe that the planet's people, with access to such sophisticated technology, weren't at least curious about each other.

Quark answered for the team, startling everyone except the captain. "Why do you think we call them 'Natives'? It's because they don't even have a generic name for themselves. Everything is just village this and village that. . . ." Quark leaned forward and spoke in a conspiratorial whisper, glancing at the disheartened villagers as if afraid they would overhear and cut off his lobes. "And *they don't even have intervillage trade.* Can you believe it? It's the basis for mercantilism, which must precede capitalism—they don't even have the concept of money!"

"Money isn't everything, Quark," said Odo, curling his lip in disgust.

"But indeed it is something, Constable," said the captain. "Quark has an unhappy point. On Earth, it was merchants following trade routes who eventually converted isolated city-states into great nations."

Quark picked up the thread, surprising even Captain Sisko with his sudden earnestness; the subject was clearly dear to his Ferengi heart. "These Natives are living in a *posteconomic* society. . . . Everything they need, they literally find scattered on the ground like dead leaves. They've never had to *trade* for anything in their lives.

"They don't understand the concept of making things or the division of labor or the accumulation of capital to finance large-scale projects. How do you expect them to learn it all in an eye blink? And if they don't, what makes you think they won't just wander off in the middle of one of Chief O'Brien's engineering lectures?"

"And if the enemy just repeats their sneak attack," said the chief, "clicking off the broadcast power to a village, then attacking it, over and over, then the Natives will panic, and their villages are going to fall, one by one, until the Cardassians control every Native settlement on the planet. I don't have to tell you what that means."

Indeed he didn't; Sisko thought of all he had learned about the brutal occupation of Bajor—and that was when the natural cruelty of the occupiers was tempered by the frequent revolts and rebellions of the Bajorans. With such helpless slaves, the captain shuddered to think of the depths of depravity that might occur.

"Perhaps we ought to send a subspace message calling for backup," suggested Odo.

Couldn't the Defiant simply call for help, for some Starfleet ships to drive away this Drek'la-Cardassian alliance? Dax had asked exactly the same question. This time, the answer from Captain Sisko was an abrupt "No, Constable. Think of the technology that must be in the hands of the Cardassians and Drek'la by now. We don't know what they've learned to use or mounted on their ships. At the very least, we have to learn that much before we call in Starfleet. So for now, we're on our own."

"Then it looks like we don't have any other option," the chief said. "We have to find a way to start training them to fight, however long it takes."

Sisko looked from O'Brien to Worf to Odo and even to Quark; each man's unhappy, resigned look told him what he didn't want to know. The chief had stated the consensus; he was sure that when he got Dax's full report, it would contain the same recommendation.

"We need to start by forcing them to see their own need for training," said Worf.

"My thoughts precisely. It's time, I believe, for a shakedown hike." The away team looked blank, not understanding what Sisko meant. "Get the troops in line, Mr. Worf," said the captain, surveying the tricorder topographic map he had downloaded; he studied the contour lines, trying to chart a reasonably efficient route westward. . . . Better than the pell-mell dash away from the victorious enemy—*a route rather than a rout,* he thought somewhat uncharitably. "We're about to organize the Native Scouts of Sierra-Bravo."

CHAPTER
9

THREE DAYS OF *Boy Scout hell*. Chief Miles O'Brien moaned as he massaged his aching calves; he had never quite managed to become involved in Scouting—never seen the urgency behind forty-kilometer forced marches, slogging through swamps (enthusiastically labeled "wetlands" on the tricorder map) and steamy jungles, up and down precipitous slopes, all the while trying to beat into the Natives' heads that they didn't need all that technology manna falling from heaven—they could do it themselves with lower-level but *sustainable* technology.

Worf was exhilarated, and the captain seemed chipper enough, but O'Brien found himself siding more and more with Quark; the two grumpy old men of the group didn't see anything stimulating about a huge gorge to cross or a marsh to wade through. The chief was amused, however, to watch Captain Sisko's best laid schemes gang aft a-gley.

The countryside was rugged and forbidding. The mineral composition of the soil meant the ground was spongier than on other planets, and since they were in a very moist climatic band above the planet's equator, they were inundated by water from all directions: rain, seepage, and rivers, sluggish and meandering on the plains, rushing white water in the hills. The combination of the spongy soil and seepage meant quicksand, of course, and the mineral content made it more like cement sand. Just walking was hazardous. Though the brilliant blues and greens, in trees and rocks alike, punctuated by streaks of brilliant orange-and-red algae and fungi, made for a colorful (if deadly, draining, and inedible) hike.

The planetary axis tilted alarmingly toward the sun, so the sun rose not so much in the east as the northeast, hooking around the sky in a great crescent, then setting in the northwest. Masses of clouds (more particulate precipitants in the air) acted as heat transfer engines, warming the air to an unbearable mugginess in the daytime, then dissipating to allow rapid cooling close to zero degrees Celsius at night. A real garden spot.

The overt purpose of the hike, as Sisko explained it to the Natives, was to trek across seventy-five kilometers of wilderness to reach a certain village far enough away from the enemy that the Tiffnakis (and the away team) would stay out of the invaders' way—until they were ready to return and fight. Unsurprisingly, Asta-ha and her Tiffnaki comrades were spoiling for a rematch.

"I want to immobilize them with my motion constrictor," she said, fixing the chief with a mad, rigid stare, "and slowly rip their limbs off with the lift pull, the murderers." The motion constrictor, O'Brien discovered after they got far enough away to begin picking up power broadcast from another relay, was a small, one-handed neural-impulse inhibitor; the lift pull was a phaser-sized tractor beam that required an anchor point. O'Brien had never seen either one of those two pieces of technology before in his life.

The *covert* reason for the march was to put the Tiffnakis into a position where they *had to* rely on themselves and their own ingenuity. It was Captain Sisko's idea to march them across the most forbidding landscape imaginable so they would be forced, willy-nilly, to discover three of the four basic engines of antiquity: the lever, the pulley, and the inclined plane (neither the captain nor Chief O'Brien could think of a way to introduce the Tiffnakis to the water screw). At the least, the away team expected the Natives to finally understand ropes, especially after rappelling down a cliff face. Alas, as the Scottish poet Bobbie Burns wrote, a verse that came back to O'Brien again and again:

But Mousie, thou art no thy lane,
In proving foresight may be vain:
The best laid schemes o'mice an' men,
  Gang aft a-gley,
An' lea'e us naught but grief an' pain,
  For promis'd joy!

—And the trip did not work out *quite* the way the captain planned.

The first tiny glitch occurred late the first full day of travel, when they came to the precipitous cliff face (marked on the tricorder map by an incredibly tight convergence of sixteen contour lines) down which Sisko intended them to rappel.

Looking over the face of that monstrous cliff, even O'Brien felt his gut tighten, and a chill passed from tailbone to cervical vertibrae. "We're, ah, going to rappel down that . . . sir?"

But the captain beamed, happy as a proverb. "I always feel so exhilarated when I drop down a mountain," he exclaimed. He walked away from the milling Tiffnakis, whom Worf struggled to keep from pressing close to the cliff like penguins trying to chivvy one of their number off the edge to see if it was safe. The chief watched Captain Sisko tap his combadge and speak in low tones for a moment; a few minutes later—*long enough to get to the* Defiant's *replicators and back,* thought O'Brien—eight harnesses, ropes, and anchor stakes materialized on the ground nearby—along with more edible combat rations, "com-rats," for the Federation members, who could not, of course, live off the poisonous wasteland.

Sisko returned. "The constable and Quark will demonstrate the technique . . . won't you, gentlemen?" Odo didn't look too worried; *he can shapeshift into a bird or something if he starts to fall,* thought the chief. But the Ferengi was first confused, then shocked, then horrified as Worf took Quark by the elbow and hustled him over to the rigs and ropes.

"Think of the harness as a sort of chair made of nylochite webbing," said the captain, flashing a face-splitting grin. "You basically sit in it, as Quark is demonstrating."

"What?" demanded the Ferengi, turning distinctly pink. "You were *serious?* You expect me to trust my precious life to *that* pile of primitive junk?" His eyes grew nearly as huge as his ears, and he tried to back away—only to back directly into an immovable Chief O'Brien, who had casually shifted behind the Ferengi, trapping him.

Worf steamed; he did not like the humidity one bit. "You will put on this harness," he snarled, "or I will put it on for you."

Quark breathed a sigh of relief. "Oh, would you? There's a good Klingon. You'd make a much better test subject than I."

With a howl of frustration, the Klingon surged forward, webbed harness in hand, and struggled with the Ferengi; a moment later, a yoked and harnessed Quark cringed before the mighty-thewed

Klingon warrior. "Your years of sitting behind a
bar have made you fat and sluggish," said Worf.

"I don't sit, I stand," mustered the Ferengi with
some dignity. Constable Odo, meanwhile, had
pulled on his own harness with no fuss.

"Now observe carefully," said the captain to the
fascinated Tiffnakis. He found a solid rock without
difficulty and pressed the anchor pins to the rock
surface, one by one; they phased partially out of
existence, dropping deep into the rock with hardly
any resistance; then they phased back to solid with
a bang. . . . They were embedded into place much
more strongly than could ever be the old-fashioned
kind that one pounded into a crack.

Running one end of each rope through the anchor pins, Sisko showed Asta-ha and another gag-
gle of Tiffnakis designated the "second group" how
to run the rope through the carabiners attached to
the front of the harnesses. Then Odo backed to the
edge of the cliff and began to jump, letting out rope
as he fell . . . rapidly enough for a quick descent,
but not so fast as to lose control. Quark took some
prodding by Worf; he fell jerkily, shouting and
cursing all the way until his voice faded from
earshot.

Fearless, the Tiffnakis crowded the edge of the
cliff, craning their necks to follow the progress of
the two "volunteers." 'Such tech," breathed Tivva-
ma, Asta-ha's daughter.

Odo landed on the ground and quickly shed the
harness, which Chief O'Brien hauled back up. A

few seconds later, Quark lighted, but the Ferengi just stood there shaking. "Come on, you coward!" shouted the chief. "Strip that thing off so the next batch can go." Quark stared up at the chief, silently mouthing something obscene in Ferengi. Then he pulled off the webbing (fighting off some unwanted help from Odo), and O'Brien hauled up that harness as well.

"All right, then," said Captain Sisko, striding forward with more harnesses in hand. "Where's my next batch of Scouts?"

O'Brien looked around for Asta-ha. "Well, she *was* right here," he said, puzzling over the disappearance. "Maybe she got frightened and ran off?" Suddenly, Worf shouted in surprise, pointing down the cliff face. O'Brien jumped, so startled he almost fell off. Heart pounding, he leaned over and saw Asta-ha and about twenty of her Tiffnaki villagers slowly floating down the cliff in perfect comfort . . . wearing nothing but their clothes.

Sisko, O'Brien, and Worf stared openmouthed, no one saying a word, as the Natives drifted down at a constant velocity, finally landing at the bottom with a tiny bump. Cupping her hands, Asta-ha shouted up to the Scout troop still waiting above: "Perfect. Send down the next group, Captain Sisko."

Another group was already stepping toward the cliff edge when Sisko waved them back. "How the *hell* did they *do* that?" he bellowed.

Fighting back a grin, Chief O'Brien told the

captain about the antigrav device Asta-ha had demonstrated back at the well the first time they saw her. Sisko leaned close to the chief. "This was supposed to be a learning experience," he said, patiently but with much menace behind the words. "We're supposed to be teaching the Natives how to survive *without* their technology. Confiscate all antigrav devices right now."

"Yes, sir," the chief said, "I thought we had. They must have had more."

The Tiffnakis remaining at the top of the cliff looked startled as the chief relayed the order; reluctantly, thirteen of them handed over devices ranging in size from a medical scanner to a phaser. The chief put them in a bag and handed them to the captain, who quietly had the *Defiant* beam them up. "Much better," he concluded. "Now let's get them down the cliff."

O'Brien and Worf returned to the cliff edge, but something was wrong: most of the Tiffnakis were gone—disappeared. Struck with a sudden suspicion, the chief went immediately to the cliff edge and looked over; now the Tiffnakis were descending on a slant, as if sliding down a gigantic slide. . . . But there was nothing there.

For an instant, O'Brien felt a surge of panic; he had never longed for a bottle of Tullamore Dew as much as he did just then. Then, with a sigh of relief, he recalled the force beam benches in the village; evidently, some enterprising Tiffnaki had set up a device to project such a force beam slantwise down the cliff, and the rest were simply sliding down it to the ground.

By the time the three away team members on top of the cliff located the device, all but three of the Tiffnakis were already on the beam slide. Worf and O'Brien stopped the last three, but of course they couldn't shut off the beam until the last person touched ground (not wanting to drop the sliding Tiffnakis to their deaths). Sisko confiscated the force beam generator; up it went to the ship.

"Any more force beams?" demanded the captain, his teeth grinding and fists clenching and unclenching. The remaining three Tiffnakis shook their heads. "Antigrav devices? Aircars? Parachutes?"

"What's a parachute?" asked one of the remaining three.

O'Brien jumped in to explain, while the captain cooled off for a moment. "A piece of material shaped like, um, a dome or hemisphere, which catches the air and lowers you gently when you fall."

A Tiffnaki brightened. "Oh. That's right, I almost forgot." Before anyone could stop him, he walked to the edge and stepped off. Sure enough, when O'Brien stared downward, there was the telltale blue billow as the native wafted gently down the cliff, like a dead leaf falling from an autumn branch.

Sisko lunged forward, grabbing each of the remaining two Tiffnakis by the scruff of his collar.

One was Owena-da, the man who had handed out the weapons before the disastrous fight against the Cardassians; O'Brien didn't know the other one. "Get-in-the-harnesses," enunciated Captain Sisko, hands shaking with suppressed emotion.

Confused by the captain's obvious rage, the two Tiffnakis quickly complied, stepping into the webbed affairs alongside Worf, O'Brien, and the captain himself. The chief swiftly planted three more anchor pins for a total of five, one for each of them.

"Walk to the edge backwards," said Sisko, back in control of himself, "and step off."

O'Brien turned around and demonstrated, as did Worf on the other side of the Tiffnakis. O'Brien tried to keep his right hand clear, in case he had to reach out and grab a Whatsit, should one panic and lose control of the rope.

The captain was still giving helpful advice: "Lean back against the rope and let it play out. . . . Slowly, there's no—" Sisko froze in midsentence, as both Tiffnakis had simply backed off the cliff with no hands and begun to plummet.

Leaping wildly, O'Brien struggled to catch up with the Natives, who were simply falling at normal gravitational acceleration, their ropes slack; then the chief pulled up short as he abruptly caught up with them: they had come to a sudden halt—*but their ropes were still slack.* They started to descend once more, lowering at a constant speed while still not holding their ropes; it was as if they were being lowered by an invisible fishing line attached to a reel on top of the cliff. The chief bounced closer, straining to see if there was a wire; what he saw instead was that each Whatsit had his hands cupped, as if holding something.

At that moment, O'Brien remembered the hand-held "tractor beam" toy that Owena-da had shown him. He sighed deeply and bounced the remaining distance to the ground in one mighty leap.

When the captain touched ground minutes later, he may as well have been wearing a sign that said "Abandon hope all ye who talk to me." O'Brien touched his combadge and quietly said, "O'Brien to anchor pins: release." The ropes went suddenly slack, and the freed anchor pins dropped to the ground, bouncing a couple of times on the hard, mineral-rich surface.

Wordlessly, Captain Sisko stormed off along his preplanned route, not even bothering to collect the handheld tractor beams. . . . The commander and the chief took it upon themselves to confiscate the cheat-tools and send them upstairs.

"Well, sir," said O'Brien cheerfully, five kilometers later, "what's next on the outdoorsman's test?"

Captain Sisko had cooled off his own temper by leading the Scout mob on a fast march: five klicks at six and a half kilometers per hour. It would have been a fast walk along a paved road; in the wilderness, it was more like an overland run. Fortunately for O'Brien (and the only point that kept poor Quark alive), the planet had a gravitational acceleration only 0.79 that of Federation standard. . . . It was like the chief had dropped sixteen kilograms, or more than two stone. The Tiffnakis were huffing and blowing so much, it sounded like a balloon-inflating contest. Neither Worf nor the captain was even sweating heavily; nor Odo, of course, but he didn't count.

Sisko consulted his tricorder map, smiling faintly in a way that raised snakes in O'Brien's stomach. "Dead ahead is a marsh that preliminary tricorder readings put at about a meter deep, with the approximate consistency of tar."

"Oh, lovely. This is a really . . . challenging course you've laid in for us, Captain." The chief didn't mind physical exercise, when it was *fun,* like stretching himself against Dr. Bashir at springball. But slogging through a sticking bog, with tendrils of goo that clung to every step like the vengeful dead resenting the footsteps of the living, was decidedly not Miles Edward O'Brien's idea of a grand time.

"Scout troop, halt," ordered the captain; Worf relayed the order up and down the line of two hundred in a series of bellows that could probably be heard by Dax up in orbit. O'Brien stared at the vast expanse of nothingness ahead of them. The marsh (bog, fen, swamp, mud hole) stretched as far as his eye could see . . . a blue black sea of frozen waves and humps that were probably sandbars of relative solidity. *Then again, knowing the captain, they might be bottomless dust bowls,* thought O'Brien; he decided to give leadership its privilege of going first.

"Well, troops," addressed the captain, "I will leave it up to your ingenuity to get yourselves across this mess. You're going to have to know how to traverse such terrain if you want to fight a guerrilla war against the—against your invaders." Sisko turned back to the mob, jabbing his finger at Asta-ha, then rotating to include all the Tiffnakis in the admonition: "And there shall be *no* use of force beams, parachutes, paragliders, or antigravitational devices of *any sort.* Is that understood?"

"Why not?" asked the hereditary mayor in puzzlement. "If the tech gives us the means to cross this smelly and unpalatable fen, why shouldn't we use it?"

O'Brien responded for the captain. "Don't you remember what happened in the battle? The invaders have the capability to make all your lovely tech stop working. What are you going to do when your antigravs fail, and you're a hundred meters in the sky?"

Asta-ha nodded sagely; her little girl Tivva-ma imitated her with tremendous gravity. "Yes, I see your point," admitted the mother. "No antigravs, or anything else that could injure or kill us if the tech suddenly chose to take itself away."

The Tiffnakis called a town meeting to discuss the new, perplexing rules, and Sisko gestured the away team away to allow the villagers to work out their own problem. The captain sucked in a lungful, looking upon the slough of despair as if it were a rolling line of modest hills under a soft carpet of Bajoran *dushti* grass. "This takes me back," he said. "One thing I find I miss as commanding officer is the opportunity to lead an away team: just me and my command against the elements. It's invigorating."

Odo was staring at the mob of Scouts. "It also appears to be exfoliating," he said.

"What?" asked Sisko. "Constable, if you could be a bit more . . ." The captain trailed off, and O'Brien followed Sisko's gaze.

The Tiffnakis, led by Asta-ha, were just finishing burning a path arrow-straight through the swamp, using a projection device that strongly resembled an old-fashioned coffee grinder, including the hand crank. The mayor was using the crank as the away team watched, playing an orange beam up and down the new path . . . a rock-hard rut with permanent sides that appeared to be—

"Obsidian," breathed the chief.

"Volcanic glass," responded Constable Odo automatically. *Probably wondering if he can shapeshift into it,* thought O'Brien.

"This is completely unacceptable!" shouted the Klingon, but the captain merely sighed and shook his head.

"I can see this just isn't going to work," he said sadly; "I have a very bad feeling about this."

Asta-ha put the finishing touches on her creation, and with a wave, the Tiffnakis began marching normal-pace along the hardened furrow she had dug; at the rate they were trucking, O'Brien figured they would be at the other side of the bog in thirty minutes . . . without a spoiled shoe or muddied pant leg in the lot.

Chief O'Brien heard an abrupt cry for help from twenty meters away in the opposite direction; it was Quark, who seemed to be the only person floundering in the swamp for some peculiar reason. *In the SWAMP?* puzzled the chief.

Odo led the pack over to his old sparring partner. "What's the matter, Quark? Did you go swimming too soon after stuffing your face?"

"Get—me—*OUT!*" shrieked the Ferengi, panicked.

For some reason, everyone turned and looked at O'Brien. "Well, how come *I* have to dive in and get covered with that foul-smelling mud?" Nobody answered, but nobody else volunteered, either. "Oh, all right. Why not? Clearly it's the job of the senior chief to wade into the mud hole to rescue any random bartenders we happen to find."

"Chief, *HELP!* I'm dying, I'm dying!"

O'Brien scanned with his tricorder. "Oh for God's sake, Quark, it's only a meter deep—just stand up."

"I can't. I'm—my coat is too heavy!"

The chief waited a few moments, expecting Quark to stop whining and get up, but it became obvious that the Ferengi was struggling against a heavy weight, like a huge pair of hands rising from the mud to suck him down. "Chief," said the captain, "I think you ought to see to your team-mate."

O'Brien rolled his eyes, but Sisko had a point: having accepted Quark onto the away team, they had to treat him like a normal member. Sighing in exasperation, Chief O'Brien waded into the goo, stepping gingerly to avoid slipping and falling. He struggled his way to Quark. "How the hell did you get out here?" he demanded, trying to get a grip on the Ferengi's mud-soaked jacket.

"I slipped and kept sliding," snarled Quark. "What did you think, that I was *swimming* to the opposite shore?"

"What have you been eating? You weigh a ton, Quark."

The Ferengi looked simultaneously smug and put-upon. "I'll thank you to keep your personal comments to yourself," he sniffed.

Something felt strange—wrong. "In fact," mused the chief, "it's *not* you what's so heavy . . . it's your damned jacket!"

"W-w-what do you mean? How could a jacket be heavy?"

Quark tried so hard to look casual that O'Brien instantly grew suspicious. Reaching around Quark from behind, the chief yanked the jacket off the Ferengi with a swift move. Sure enough, the garment weighed nearly twenty kilos.

Quark popped up immediately, now jacketless and no longer mired. "Give it back!" he shrieked, snatching for the coat. "You have no right—*it's mine!*"

"There's something in here," announced the chief, holding the jacket aloft with one hand, just out of Quark's reach.

"It's mine. I found it."

"Now now, Quark," said Odo, striding into the mud to intercede between the struggling pair; he removed the jacket from O'Brien's hand and held it aloft himself. . . . Three meters aloft. "You wanted to be part of the away team? Well, now you are. . . . So whatever you found belongs to the Federation."

O'Brien quickly looked at the Tiffnakis, but they were long out of sight; Odo had been careful not to let them see him shapeshifting. . . . "One shock at a time," the constable explained.

"Why don't you bring that coat out here," suggested Captain Sisko. "We can all take a look and see what wonderful thing Mr. Quark has found."

Constable Odo slooshed his way onto the bank; O'Brien let go the Ferengi and followed, leaving Quark to struggle his way out unassisted. The chief stared at Odo; naturally, the changeling's "trousers" were still sparkling clean, since they weren't cloth at all but Odo's own body cells. O'Brien and especially Quark looked as though they had been dunked in an inkwell.

Laying the jacket out on the ground, Odo began

searching each pocket. *"Hey,"* shouted Quark, rallying for one last defense of his privacy, "don't you need a search warrant?"

The constable smiled condescendingly at him. "Not to safety-check the equipment of a member of the *away team,* surely." Odo pulled packet after packet out of Quark's pockets, laying them on the ground at the Ferengi's feet.

O'Brien bent and studied them. "Dirt," he pronounced, pouring it into his hand and sifting it through his fingers; it felt cool, crumbly, and faintly metallic. "Quark, why in God's name did you fill your pockets with dozens of bags of *dirt?"*

The Ferengi said nothing, but Odo rolled his eyes disgustedly. "He didn't fill his pockets with dirt. . . . He *lined* his pockets with latinum— latinum drops."

Quark snarled at the ground, saying nothing lest it be taken down in evidence and used against him. Worf snarled and edged closer to the Ferengi; O'Brien thought the Klingon looked like he was hoping to get in one good shot before Captain Sisko could stop him.

"So, Mr. Quark," said the captain, defusing the situation with a smile, "I see you've been collecting geological samples. Not a bad idea. Let's send them up to the *Defiant* for analysis." He touched his combadge: "Sisko to *Defiant."*

Silence. The captain tried a hail again, then added, "Dax, are you there?" There was no response.

Feeling suddenly apprehensive and very much alone, O'Brien slapped his own badge. "O'Brien to Dax—Commander, can you hear us?" The response was the same: nothing. Worf, Odo, and even Quark tried with no better luck.

O'Brien whipped up his tricorder, dialed the scan range out to maximum, and swept the sky. "Captain," he said slowly, hardly believing his own words as they came out his mouth, "it's gone."

"Gone?" Sisko didn't seem to understand.

"Gone. The *Defiant,* it's gone—it's no longer in orbit."

"Dax," said Worf, with a sudden and very personal apprehension; he got hold of himself immediately, turning to the captain. "Perhaps the Cardassian ships discovered the *Defiant,* and Commander Dax took it out of orbit."

O'Brien checked again. "No, there's no warp signature; nobody has used warp engines around here since we arrived. She's just . . ."—he looked up—"gone, Captain." *Taking our future luncheons and suppers with her,* he thought.

A pensive Captain Sisko absently rubbed his beard and stared after the Tiffnakis. "Gentlemen," he said at last, "this is no longer a Scouting hike. This is now a military action. And like it or not, *those*"—he gestured at the trail burned through the mud—"are our only forces." Then he turned back to the team and grinned. "Let's see just how much hell we can give," he said, grinning like a Klingon general.

I should be scared out of my wits, thought the chief, but he didn't feel frightened: he felt the most curious sense of liberation. At last, a chance to scratch the itch that had bothered him ever since the Cardassians had defected from the war to join the Dominion; *a real hullabaloo, and no holds barred.* "Too bad we don't have any Tullamore Dew," he muttered, but nobody heard him.

CHAPTER
10

LIEUTENANT COMMANDER Jadzia Dax sat in the *Defiant*'s lonely command chair—lonely not only because all her comrades were down on the planet below, but because she felt she should be with them. Julian said her wound was healing nicely, and that she'd be ready to fight in another day or two, but that meant nothing now.

Stupid, she berated herself, *fretting won't help them.* She tried to keep a poker face for the duty shift on the bridge, Ensigns Weymouth and N'Kduk-Thag (with a glottal stop; Dax couldn't quite pronounce it) and Lieutenant junior grade Joson Wabak, a good-looking Bajoran man that made Jadzia think fondly of her wilder days. Curzon had had lots of "relationships" that he'd given little long-term thought to, but in her female years Dax had rarely been quite that frivolous.

Suddenly, Lieutenant Wabak at Ops jumped in startlement and stared intensely at his threat board. "Commander," he said hesitantly, "we were just scanned."

Dax considered. "Random sweeps by the Cardassian ships. Right?"

"No, ma'am." Wabak looked up nervously. "We're being scanned by the planet."

"By the *planet?*" Dax half rose. "By the Natives? Or is it a Cardassian probe?"

"I mean scanned by the planetary defense system in orbit. . . . *Not* the Cardassian ship, ma'am."

Uh oh. . . . Dax almost sprinted to the threat board. Looking over the lieutenant's shoulder, she double-checked his read. He was absolutely right: the scan came from orbit, and it wasn't a Cardassian signal-processing system.

Dax uttered a single Klingon oath before she remembered she was in charge: raw ensigns (and jaygees) did not want to hear their commanding officer get upset. "All right, so we've been detected by the planetary defense systems; they're not firing on the Cardassians. . . . Any reason to think they'll fire on us?"

"Well," hedged Wabak, "we are a lot closer than they are."

"Mr. Wabak, how much higher in orbit are the Cardassians?"

"We're at half-synchronous, about forty-three thousand. The Cardassians are all somewhere around a hundred thousand kilometers."

Ensign N'Kduk-Thag cleared his throat; it sounded like sandpaper across a washboard. "The Cardassians would doubtless prefer to be at a much closer orbit to support their troops," he said, speaking perfectly correctly but without inflection.

"Or even at the one percent atmospheric level, to cover the entire planet more quickly," added Wabak, "like a low orbit with a one- or two-hour period." Ensign Weymouth said nothing; she sort of contracted within herself—earning a possible "down" on her OOD watch, whenever Dax got around to doing the CDO log.

"In either case," continued the monotone of Ensign N'Kduk-Thag, "the Cardassian ships would not be so far away from the planet's surface unless they were afraid of being detected and classified as an unfriendly object by something—presumably the planetary defenses."

The opening salvo of *something* struck them at just that moment. "Incoming," shouted Lieutenant Wabak, somewhat belatedly.

There was no shock; the *Defiant* didn't rock or shudder. The beam that struck them was nondestructive, fortunately—since of course they had no shields. They were "silent running," as the Trill recalled submariners used to call it centuries ago; the cloak was incompatible with shields.

"Shields up," said Wabak.

Without a perceptible pause, Commander Dax responded, "Belay that. Ensign Weymouth, diagnostics. . . . What the hell is the beam doing to us? Anything? Is it a scan?"

The brunette—whose hair was shaved into some improbable design that was probably a religious symbol (otherwise Starfleet wouldn't allow it)—squeaked nervously, but her hands flew across the console. *Once you kick her in the butt, she's not too bad,* thought Dax abstractly, editing the log entry in her head. "It's, um, not doing anything. I mean, I don't see any problems."

"Try a level-three."

"I did, levels two through five. No damage, sir."

"Wabak? N'Kduk-Thag? Sorry if I mangled your name. . . . Can I call you Nick?"

"You may call me Nick. Commander, I can detect no effect from the beam."

"Neither can . . ." Wabak trailed off, staring at his threat board with eyes so bright blue, Dax idly wondered whether they would shine in the dark. A pity he hadn't come aboard *Deep Space Nine* a year earlier. . . .

"What is it, Wabak?"

"The Cardassians are scanning us—and they're heading right toward us."

Dax was up and out of the command chair again, looking over Wabak's shoulder, vaguely aware it probably wasn't a good idea—it might make him think she lacked confidence in him. "Now what?

How are they . . . Weymouth, fire a probe, opposite direction from the Cardassians."

The ensign poked at her board, Dax heard a faint hiss. "Probe away."

"Point it backwards and take a look at us on sensors; put it on the main viewer."

Five pairs of eyes on the bridge, counting the silent security chief by the turbolift, stared up at the main viewer. Dax saw a star field, with a pair of dots moving slowly closer; each dot was accompanied by a bright green box full of information about the type and specs of Cardassian warship it was. But the centerpiece of the screen was a giant-sized picture of the *Defiant,* accompanied by its own bright green box . . . and the ship was radiating on all frequencies.

"So much for the cloak," said Dax, more disappointed than incredulous. "No *wonder* we're attracting attention. We're lit up like a courting lantern."

"Well," said Lieutenant Wabak weakly, "at least now we know what the planetary-defense beam does, Commander."

"Belay that last belay, Lieutenant. Shields, quickly—before the Cardassians get close enough to take a clean shot."

"Incoming torpedo from the cruiser," said Wabak, raising shields, but the shot was far wide, of course. . . . They were only barely in range.

"Ensign Weymouth, evasive maneuvers."

"Which—which pattern should I use, sir?"

"Pattern four."

The *Defiant* began to bob and weave, maneuvering to keep the planet in between herself and the Cardassians . . . an impossible task, Dax quickly realized, as the seven ships fanned out: the two GM-class heavy cruisers, either of which could probably handle the *Defiant* by itself, backed away, waiting for the cruiser and the four destroyers to harass and chivvy the Federation vessel, which had probably been identified by then, into the open. Dax felt herself begin to sweat, feeling like a burglar when someone suddenly turned on all the lights.

"Commander—should we contact the away team?"

"Negative. The Cardassians will just follow the signal—"

"And they will locate the away team," finished the unpronounceable Ensign Nick.

Please Benjamin, she prayed silently, *whatever you do, DON'T call me right now.*

The *Defiant* lurched with another disruptor torpedo, fired this time by one of the destroyers; it was only a small charge, and not a direct shot in any event, but Dax realized it was the harbinger of more, many more, to come.

"Commander!" shouted Wabak. "Should we return fire?"

"Don't bother," she said, glumly.

"What?"

"Don't bother returning fire, we're out of effective range. Weymouth, continue evasive maneuvers. . . . Do it randomly—use the computer, that's what it's there for." Dax paced nervously, aware she was showing her stress, hoping it would just appear as battle lust. *It would make sense; over the last few centuries, they know I've been a berserker warrior more than once.*

"Incoming," said the jaygee. "Torpedo, two disruptor blasts—took us on . . . the disruptors took us on the for'ard left flank, shields holding."

"Sort of," added Dax, noticing the bridge lights flicker . . . a subtle sign of power strain as the computer instantly compensated.

"Return fire?"

"We're not close enough, Lieutenant; just vamp until ready."

"What?"

"Sorry. . . . Just fly in circles, try to keep the planet between us and the heavies." Centuries ago, on ancient Earth, when the vaudeville acts weren't quite ready but the audience were restive, the MC would "vamp until ready"—come out, tell jokes, sing songs, insult the audience, and in general make a *tummel,* literally a noise, until the first juggler or dance act felt the psychic moment was perfect to make an appearance (or was paid the extortion money they demanded not to walk off the show). At the moment, against two heavy dreadnoughts and five smaller ships, that was about all the *Defiant* could do—and Dax knew it. The junior officers should have known it too, but Jadzia Dax was more willing to forgive the sins of youth than her youthful protégé, Benjamin Sisko.

Suddenly, Lieutenant Wabak jumped half out of his chair and his skin. *"Incoming missiles!"* he nearly screamed; then without bothering to ask permission, he fired a pair of photon torpedoes. The explosion literally *spun the ship,* sending it tumbling in its orbit until Ensign Weymouth corrected and regained control.

"What the hell was that?" demanded the commander.

"Planetary defenses," bellowed Wabak, trying to regain control of himself. "Prophets, more missiles."

"Get us out of this orbit, Mister."

Discussion ceased as the bridge crew poured on the impulse engines, increasing momentum in the direction of their orbit; in accordance with gravitational laws that not even the Joint Federation, Klingon, and Cardassian Peace Negotiations Discussion Subcommittee could yet repeal, the *Defiant* drifted farther and farther from the center of the planet. "Take out any missiles aimed at us," ordered Dax retroactively, for the record. The lieutenant junior grade repeated his earlier actions, though this time one of the missiles got too close, and the explosion tore right through the shields and shredded the external packet of one of the nacelles.

"Dax to Bashir. Casualties on decks, ah, nine and

ten." The battle continued, forces conjoined, and Dax forgot everything, even the casualties, in her mad zeal somehow to keep the rest of them alive for at least a few more minutes.

Dr. Bashir, running down a corridor in the increasingly damaged *Defiant*, staggered and fell against the bulkhead as the damned ship heaved and shook under the bombardment. He barely avoided actually sprawling on the deck and dropping everything.

A nurse behind him unnecessarily grabbed him under the arms and helped him up. "I'm all *right*, Aaastaak," he snapped, testy under the strain.

Julian Bashir sighed as he continued down the corridor, slower this time. *Well, this IS what I signed up for, isn't it?* "A lesser man would crumble," he muttered, but Virjaaj Aaastaak didn't hear, of course: Toorjaani were known throughout the quadrant for their lousy hearing, made up for by an almost psychic empathy with the injured, nearly as good as the Betazoids'. Taking a break from bumpy noses, evolution had equipped the Toorjaani with noses that bent at a right angle, pointing left (the dominant caste) or right (servants, doormen, boot polishers, so on); the Federation had debated their admission for years.

And here I am, mentally babbling again, thought the doctor angrily. Bashir pushed through an emergency door that was flashing red; had it been flashing blue, it would have indicated hull breach beyond it, and Dr. Bashir would have needed a pressure suit to treat the casualties—assuming they managed to survive a close encounter with the Void.

And casualties there were. Sixteen crewmen were scattered about the room, bloodstains painted the floor an eerie red with streaks of green (Vulcan) and silver and black (any of several different species; Bashir would worry about identifcation after triage). *"Aaastaak!"* shouted the doctor, catching the Toorjaani's attention. *"Her and her, emergency transport to sickbay. The ones I'm marking get your immediate attention."* The ship rocked again, throwing Bashir to his knees. *What the hell is going on up there?* he wondered, climbing back to his feet.

As the two most injured crewwomen disappeared into sparkles, Bashir drew a device from his bag and spray-painted the faces of seven other crewmen: they all had broken bones, multiple contusions, and serious but not life-threatening lacerations and abrasions; one was bleeding badly enough that the doctor staunched the flow before spraying him. *"Leave the rest until later. They can wait."*

Bashir slapped his combadge. *"Marge. Start . . ."* Realizing he was still shrieking like a banshee, Bashir cleared his aching throat and started over. "Marge, prep the two patients for immediate surgery, then start with an alpha wave inducer and start isolating the most serious internals with an exoscalpel. I'll be down in three or four minutes." He was holding tight to a hatch-access handle; nevertheless, he was almost knocked off his feet anyway when the ship first lurched forward, like a boat sliding down a particularly grim wave, then jumped backwards, as if it had slammed into something solid (like a planet).

Leaving Aaastaak in charge of the first serious casualty site, Julian Bashir picked up his tricorder and medical bag and literally ran to the next chamber. He found only four more casualties, none as seriously injured as the ensign and the patient he had already sent to surgery. "People, listen up," he said. "You can all make it next door except you, Ensign. The rest of you go into that room there"—Bashir pointed—"and the nurse will take care of you after he squares away some other, more seriously wounded patients."

Bashir pressed his lips together, playing his portable plasma infusion unit across the chest of the far more seriously injured Ensign Yamada, who had lost a significant amount of blood. The ship seemed to roll; at least Julian Bashir was pressed against the floor with nearly three times the normal gravitation allowed by the inertial dampers.

"Ensign Jones," he gasped when he could breathe again, "I checked you out: your pulse, respiration, and blood pressure are all normal. Whatever you're feeling is entirely in your mind; your body is all right, except for some minor scratches." Dr. Bashir looked up at the sweating, shaky starman. "It's all right to be scared—I'm scared to death. You're going to be fine, . . . trust me. I *am* a doctor." He smiled at the man, who looked terribly embarrassed at his outburst.

When Bashir had stopped Yamada's blood flow with his hypotourniquet, despite being knocked to his rear twice because of torpedoes or disruptors pounding against the fading shields, the doctor had the computer transport himself directly to sickbay. Just as he arrived, the ship rolled so severely that the inertial dampers couldn't quite keep up; Bashir found himself hanging from the edge of the operating table, while the bulkhead separating the surgery from his office abruptly became the "floor." Then normal gravity reasserted itself, and he fell to the deck.

He stood, holding his stomach and trying to find the breath that had been knocked away by the blow. "Oh, Marge . . . this is going to be a relaxing session." He shook his numbed arm. "I can just feel it in my bones."

The nurse looked at Bashir and shook her head, as if ruing the day she had ever been assigned to Dr. Julian Bashir.

Jadzia Dax was far too busy to be sick to her stomach; after the third time thrown to the deck, she sat in the command chair and ordered everyone, herself included, to strap in. It was the most lopsided battle she had fought in more than a century: the *Defiant* had been so busy dodging, she had gotten off only a few, poorly aimed shots at the

Cardassian attackers . . . and those had done barely any damage at all.

"Weymouth, continue evasive maneuvers. Wabak, shoot anything you see, keep us outside the planetary defenses—last thing we need is to be dodging their impulse missiles in addition to torpedoes and disruptors." She tapped her combadge; "Dax to Ensign Nick, private channel."

She started to correct herself and use his actual name; surprisingly, N'Kduk-Thag responded instantly. . . . *The computer must have been listening to us,* mused the Trill.

"Nick, you're the only one not engaged in keeping us alive: I need input. We're being pounded. . . . Got any suggestions?" She spoke quietly into the ether, not wanting to distract either of the other two bridge officers; they had their hands full dodging Cardassians.

"We must exit the vicinity," suggested the emotionless, or at least uninflected, Ensign Nick.

"Yes, but how do we disengage when we're surrounded by Cardassians? Before we made a move in any direction, the minute their sensors picked up the impulse engine run-up, they'd be all over us like—well, never mind." She wrinkled her nose at the image she had been about to invoke.

"Then there is only one course. We must surrender the ship," concluded the rational but not exactly morale-boosting ensign. "Surely the Cardassians are more interested in capturing and studying the *Defiant* than blowing her to pieces."

Dax thought for a moment: something as yet inchoate floated in her stomach, reaching pale tendrils of cognition up her throat toward her brain. *Something . . . something there. . . .* Suddenly she knew what to do. "Ensign Nick," she called sharply, "open a channel to the lead ship—well, either of the ships. Use the Cardassian guard frequency, ah"—Dax closed her eyes for a moment and felt the nausea she had fought off so far—"twenty-seven, thirteen, thirteen, thirty, three-niner."

"Channel open, Commander."

"This is Lieutenant Commander Dax, commanding officer of the United Federation of Planets vessel *Defiant*. I hereby surrender my ship and crew and demand you cease fire in accordance with the Uniform Rules of Warfare Treaty."

The rest of the bridge crew fell silent, nearly forgetting to dodge the final incoming hammer blows.

CHAPTER
11

THE *DEFIANT* took six more hits to the shields, then the Cardassian ships grew silent; everyone drifted along his previous course, eyeballing each other. "Shields down to eleven percent," said Ensign Nick, science duty officer, doing the analysis that really should have been performed by Ensign Weymouth, "extensive hull and bioelectrical damage on most decks, atmospheric containment still operable, thirty-seven casualties—two fatal, six critical. Doctor Bashir has commenced medical treatment reports."

Weymouth and Wabak stared back at the Trill, and Joson Wabak's mouth was open in astonishment. "We're *surrendering?*" he demanded, incredulous.

"Sure sounded like it, didn't it?" Dax wasn't being intentionally cryptic; she sometimes conceived a plan and concealed it even from her own conscious mind.

A cautious voice responded over the comm link. "I am Captain Maqak. The New Cardassia accepts your surrender."

The *New* Cardassia? That wasn't a name Dax had ever heard before. "We await further instructions, Captain Maqak," said the commander. She caught Ensign Nick's eye and drew her finger across her throat; he understood and severed the connection. "Lieutenant," Dax said, leaning forward conspiratorally, "cut the shields, but let them kind of flicker out, like they were failing."

"That won't be hard," Wabak responded, eyes cold and dark.

Damn Bajorans, thought Dax, *always so emotional about everything.*

Wabak's hands were shaking with suppressed anger, frustration, humiliation, as he killed the shields.

"Are the Cardassians surrounding us?" asked Dax.

"Pretty much, *ma'am,*" he said, rolling his eyes.

"Perfect. Weymouth, listen close: just tap the impulse engines a tad, just enough to nudge us so that we pass very close on the lee side of this dreadnought here." Dax unbuckled and strode to the ensign's console, pointing at the nearest of the two larger ships.

"The—lee side, Commander?" She looked puzzled; the term was too ancient to be familiar to her, . . . a problem a multi-lived Trill had more often than one might think.

"Just get that dreadnought between us and the source of that discovery beam from the planetary defenses, Ensign. . . . You follow? I want us in Maqak's shadow, far as the beam is concerned."

Jadzia Dax glanced over at Wabak, the cute but hotheaded young Bajoran. The look of growing comprehension on his face was music.

Ensign Weymouth seemed to get it as well. She expertly maneuvered the crippled *Defiant* into position, even allowing her to tilt alarmingly, as if she had lost control of her attitude stabilizers.

"Let me know when the discovery beam is blocked," said Dax to Wabak, who stared intently at his threat board.

"But Commander," queried the greenish blue Ensign Nick, whose literality seemed to slow him down at times, "even if we restore the cloaking device will not the beam simply find us again and strip it away?"

"Out here? We're obviously beyond the triggering distance, or else they'd be shooting at the Cardassians."

"Commander, the beam is blocked," shouted Wabak.

"Joson, ready to cloak? Do it now." Dax waited a couple of seconds for the cloak to take full effect. "All right, Tina, *now*. Point zero seven five impulse, dive and to the right, get out from between 'em."

The engines hummed and rattled, obviously damaged. *Come on, babies, just a little more. We'll have plenty of time for repairs and coddling later— just GET US OUT OF HERE.* Unwilling to leave navigation, Dax hovered over Ensign Weymouth, gripping the chair and feeling excitement build in her gut like a nova. Dax's mouth was dry and her lips stuck together; she tried to lick them, but she had no saliva. As the *Defiant* dodged around the Cardassian hedge and broke free, she alternately clenched and unclenched her fingers on the back of Weymouth's chair.

"Nick! Are we trailing any debris, ionized tritium or gallium arsenide, anything like that?"

The ensign checked. "Yes, Commander, we are leaving a trail of tritium plasma. I will attempt to correct."

"No, leave it. . . . We want them to track us."

Wabak shot Dax a suspicious glance; Weymouth was too busy driving and Nick obeyed without question.

"Turn and head directly for the planet, maintain point zero seven five."

"What orbit?"

"No orbit. I said, *directly for the planet.*" *Oh boy,* she thought, *if this doesn't work . . . well, at least I won't ever have to see Benjamin staring reproachfully at me ever again.*

The *Defiant* turned and dove directly for the

planet, as Dax ordered. "Cardassians," shouted the commander.

Joson Wabak checked his threat board; for an untrained crew of junior officers, they actually weren't doing half bad, Dax realized. . . . At the back of her mind, she was already writing the log entry: *Competent and dutiful but somewhat unoriginal.* "Hope I get a chance to log it," she said under her breath.

"They're—ah—they're kind of milling around; they're sweeping the area for a warp signature."

"Hah. Well, we're not running."

"Now they're fanning out—they're heading lower. I think we're . . ."

"What? We're *what?*" Dax caught hold of herself; someone had to remain levelheaded. She back into her command chair and buckled up again.

Wabak looked back at her, eyes wide. "Commander—they've spotted the ionized tritium trail. They are tracking us. They're following us down. They'll see right where we're going!"

Dax grinned like the Cheshire Cat in that old Earth book Jake Sisko had insisted she read. "I'm counting on it. That's why we're going slow enough they can follow. Tina, set speed to one hundred kilometers per second but wait to engage for my mark."

The *Defiant* plunged closer and closer to the planet; Dax ordered Ensign Nick to count off every ten thousand kilometers, which he did a little faster than one beat per second. When they hit forty thousand kilometers from the planet, Dax said, "Tina, *engage*. Hang on, kids; Wabak, take over emergency helm—hands off, Tina—Joson, be prepared to dodge any accidental missile intercepts."

Wabak was impressed. "Oh . . . Commander, that's brilliant! Cold, but brilliant." Not surprisingly, the Bajoran seemed less than concerned about Dax's coldness toward their Cardassian attackers.

A few moments later, the pursuing Cardassians, having forgotten their lesson, also passed below forty thousand kilometers, and the planetary defenses engaged. Missiles began to launch so quickly that, even though none was fired directly at the *Defiant,* it was all Joson could do to dodge the ones headed for the targets behind.

"A hit," he shouted; since Dax hadn't felt any shudder in their own ship, she concluded he was talking about hits on the Cardassians. "Another hit. . . . Two—correct—*three* more; *Cardassian destroyer down!*" he whooped in triumph.

His triumph was short-lived, alas. "Prophets take us," he snarled, "the damned discovery beam is back."

"Found us again?"

"Yes. Now they're shooting at *us.*"

"Ten thousand," called out Ensign Nick.

"Slow up again, Wabak. Ten kilometers per second. We don't want to swat the ocean like a bullet." As they approached the great northern ocean, Dax had them slow again, and again, until finally they approached the water at a stately five hundred meters per second. Wabak continued to dodge missiles, which became tougher every time the speed dropped.

Dax touched her combadge. "Dax to crew: crash positions. Repeat, crash positions—everyone strapped in or down on the deck. Julian, put a stasis around the patients and *get down.*"

"Aye, aye, Commander."

"How close, Commander?" Joson asked nervously.

"Stay the course, Wabak."

"We're headed right for the water."

"Stay the course, Lieutenant. We're headed right *into* the water. Hang on, everybody. Count it, Nick."

"Five seconds until impact . . ." He paused; Dax held her breath, gripping the arms of the command chair, wondering for a moment whether it wasn't all just a mirage.

It struck—hard. The inertial dampers couldn't cushion the entire blow, and Dax felt a tremendous impact against the restraint webbing, which almost jerked her eyeballs out of her head. Her head snapped forward savagely, and her arms and legs splayed out in front of her.

When she blinked back to full consciousness, she made the mistake of shaking her head to clear her vision; the pain in her neck was so severe, she almost cried out. But she gritted her teeth, playing Klingon, and made no noise.

Still, with every movement of her body, especially her head and neck, Dax lurched just slightly off balance, her brain compensating for too much motion. A frightening feeling: not quite the spinning room of vertigo or the inability to stand still of dizziness, but the imbalance frightened her enough that her heart pounded. Within a few minutes, the horrible sensation coalesced into an angry pain in her neck, and she realized it was caused by the sudden jolt of the ship's impact against the sea surface.

The *Defiant* rolled and pitched far beneath the ocean waves, caught by deep underwater currents. Out the forward viewer, all the commander saw was a swirl of gradually dimming silvery blue and millions of green-glowing bubbles. "Computer," she gasped, "color correct for water transparency."

Now she jumped in vertigo, causing her head to throb as if someone were kicking her brainpan with an iron-shod boot: the ship was headed straight for an immense rock wall. She blinked, and realized it was the ocean floor; they were still pointed directly downward, though their speed was tremendously diminished—the impulse engines ran at the same power level as if they were in vacuum, but the enormous drag of seawater slowed their progress to a crawl.

Well, good, she thought; *otherwise, we might've*

smacked into the dirt before we even recovered from crashing the surface.

"Ensign Nick—what's our depth?"

"We are at one thousand one hundred meters below the surface; the pressure against the hull is one hundred and ten atmospheres, still descending; ocean floor in five hundred meters."

"Is the hull going to cave?"

"The hull is not built for high external pressure."

"Wabak, full power to the hull integrity shields. . . . In fact, overcrank it; I better head down to engineering to pump it up a bit. Tina, land us on the ocean floor and maintain the cloak." She unbuckled and stood. "Good job, crew; we made it. We're safe." She didn't add the caveat she thought silently to herself: *Safe FOR NOW.* How long "now" would be was open to consideration, . . . depending on whether she could goose the hull-integrity field to withstand an eventual hundred and sixty atmospheres of pressure from the surrounding seawater longer than a few minutes.

Otherwise . . . Dax left the bridge for the turbo-lift with visions of a fist crushing an egg, splattering the contents across the deckplates and the overhead.

Quark squatted on the frigid ground, trying not to think of hundreds, thousands of bars worth of raw latinum buried beneath his feet. *Focus,* he ordered himself; *greed is eternal; even a blind man can recognize the glow of latinum; home is where the heart is . . . but the stars are made of latinum.* The Ferengi couldn't help smiling, though his students couldn't possibly see him in the dark, despite the moons; when the immortal Seventy-Fifth Rule of Acquisition was writ, who could know how *literal* it would turn out to be?

Quark popped a glowtube. He and his twelve students were away in a dark part of the plain, not near one of the fires that dotted the heath; the fires were warmer, of course, but the Federations tended to circulate among them—and Quark's plans did not include the away team, and especially not Odo.

"Now these," he said, letting a pile of torn paper bits fall to the ground, "are called *money*. Chits, credits, whatever you want. Each chit represents— oh, call it twenty bars of gold-pressed latinum." *If we're going to go for it, let's go for it.*

Asta-ha, the female leader, nodded as if she understood.

"Do you know what gold-pressed latinum is?" asked Quark.

"Neg."

He sighed deeply. All right, let's start back a little farther. Suppose you wanted something you didn't have . . . say a piece of new tech; this glowtube, for instance. Now, I have a bunch in my pocket, and you want some. What do you do?"

Asta-ha puzzled for a moment; then she asked, "Could I have one of your glowtube techs, Quark?"

"Certainly, Asta-ha, but I want something in return. What will you offer me?"

Without a thought, the female extracted her force beam projector. "No. That's totally ridiculous," snarled the Ferengi, pocketing the projector. *I thought Sisko confiscated all that,* he idly wondered, feeling virtuous in removing another Tiffnaki cheating tool. "This glowtube gives you light for four hours, then it stops . . . but the force beam projector works forever. You gave up something much more useful for something of limited value. . . . That's *uneconomic.*"

"But what should I offer?" she asked, still trying to work it out.

"Just something equally valueless and temporary, like—" Quark struggled for an example; the problem was, *all* the technology on this priceless gem of a world was seemingly perfect and eternal. "Like a sandwich, or some other foodstuff. Yes, that's perfect. A meal gives you about four or five hours of sustenance; the glowtube gives you four hours of light. . . . A perfect trade. See why?"

"I guess so," said Asta-ha; she didn't look sure at all. "But what if you just ate?"

Quark beamed; the perfect straight line. "That's where this *money* comes in. It's a placeholder for the value. I give you the glowtube and you give me one of your chits; I hang onto the chit until I get hungry again. . . . Then I trade you back your chit, and you give me a sandwich. Get it?"

"Yeah . . . yeah."

"And suppose," continued the Ferengi, on a roll, "I get hungry and you're not around. Do I starve? No. I can trade the chit you gave me to *anyone else* who has food, and he'll give me an equivalent amount of food. Then *he* keeps the chit I gave him, and eventually, when he needs something from somebody else, he trades the chit for it."

In reality, Quark thought darkly, a Sierra-Bravo sandwich was just the ticket if he ever ended up destitute and an employee, and he decided to end it all; the local food was deadly poison to Ferengi and hu-man digestion.

Which raises an interesting question, he thought: *what ARE we going to eat when we run out of the despicable Federation com-rats?* There didn't seem to be an edible beetle in sight.

Rimtha-da, a burly man who didn't know his own strength, interrupted. "Money tech. This is an amazing discovery, Quark. You must show your friends, too."

The Ferengi sighed again. "No, it's not new tech, it's old tech . . . and anyone can use it. It's not like, ah, the antigrav, which is controlled by one person at a time; this tech only works if *everyone* uses it."

Quark worked with the Tiffnakis for more than an hour, all the while looking apprehensively over his shoulder for the omnipresent constable; somehow, Quark was certain, Odo would find a way to harass Quark for giving so generously of his knowledge of profitable capitalism. *No good deed ever goes unpunished,* he quoted to himself; it was the very last Rule of Acquisition, number 285, to be exact, and truer words were never spoken.

He made the Tiffnakis work with him, constructing several hundred pieces of "money" from the paper he had borrowed from Drukulu-da, the Tiffnakis' bard or recorder or historian—Quark wasn't sure which description fit the man best. After some false starts, the Ferengi had the Natives buying and selling all their possessions from one another, using the chits to mark the value. . . . It was truly a remarkable accomplishment, Quark thought, teaching these innumerate barbarians the principles of capitalism in just one hour.

Then Quark began to notice something odd. By the light of his fading glowtube, he examined one of the chits: he was sure he had seen that exact chit just a few moments before, and there were so many, they shouldn't be recycling so quickly. He shrugged it off, too busy to worry about the strange coincidence; he was involved in a difficult negotiation with Asta-ha for her mineral separator, which she had acquired by the Profits only knew what bizarre series of trades from someone else in the group.

A cynic, such as Odo, might have thought that Quark concocted the whole lesson just to get his greedy hands on the device, which would allow him to separate all the latinum from the soil compound. The Ferengi grinned. *Well, cynicism is an ugly emotion . . . but the universe is sometimes an ugly place.*

Then, trading away the useless (to Quark) anti-grav device, which could be found aplenty on *Deep Space Nine,* he received from Tivva-ma, Asta-ha's daughter, a handful of chits, among which were *three* exact duplicates of the chit Quark had just puzzled over. He stared at the four: they were identical, right down to the irregular tear along one edge, the exact style of numbering in the Tiffnakis' complex and inefficient duodecimal system, and even a stray charcoal mark on the back of each one of the papers.

Somebody, he realized with a terrible shock, *is counterfeiting chit markers.* Fingers counting automatically, Quark's mind raced: the only way to perfectly counterfeit the little slips of paper would be to use a tiny, handheld replicator . . . but the replicators on the ship and the station were huge, bulky affairs, run by the entirety of the ship's computer system. Quark felt dizzy at the prospect; imagine, a replicator he could carry in his pocket while out on a stroll—*I'll be a millionaire!* shrieked the vital greed center of his brain. The image of a million bars of gold-pressed latinum made him actually lose count of the "money" Tivva-ma was handing him.

CHAPTER
12

SHAKING FROM DESIRE, Quark initiated inquiries. "Asta-ha, have you ever seen a piece of tech—I don't know whether it's new or old—that lets you, ah, *duplicate* objects? Like if I had, oh I don't know, one of these chits, I could use the tech to make an exact copy?" Quark shrugged his shoulders, trying to look and sound casual; in the dim, green light from the glowtube, it occurred to him that no one could see him anyway.

"Never heard, never seen," said the female, shrugging right back at the Ferengi. She pointed to a female Quark had never met. "Jokka-ha keeps better track of tech than I. Try her."

Quark sidled up to Jokka-ha, a huge, strapping female who looked like she could roll the Ferengi into a ball and boot him into the Cardassian encampment. She, too, claimed never to have heard of such tech.

Jokka-ha sent him to Manna-ha, who sent him to Drukus-da, who sent him to Alba-ha, who sent him to Iniyard-da, who directed him to little Veelishdeiey-ma, and so on through a progression of more then forty Tiffnakis, until Quark was certain he was being given the royal runaround by the Hereditary Female Mayoress. But abruptly, the shuck stopped there with Tivva-ma herself. Quark cast a dirty look at the little girl's mother, but Asta-ha was obliviously involved in her own elaborate arms negotiation with Owena-da.

Tivva-ma solemnly nodded when Quark asked the by now ritual question about the "duplicating tech." "Yes, I have," she said, holding up an object the size of a hypospray.

"Can you show me?" asked Quark, tingling with excitement; he fished in the pocket of his once beautiful, now mud-ruined coat for something to test and found only a plastic-wrapped treat he had taken along and promptly forgotten. He extracted it cleverly, laying it on the ground in front of Tivva-ma: "Want some Huypyrian bee candy, little girl?" It was a sad but useful fact of biology, according to Dax's original analysis, that Ferengi food was *not* poisonous to Natives—though it did lack essential nutrients like cyanide, and they couldn't live on it.

The negotiation took another hour. During the

course of teaching the essentials of profit, many of the chits had somehow stuck to Quark's fingers. He fished them all out now, along with the force beam projector he took from Asta-ha as punishment, and several other pieces of tech he had accidentally acquired in the course of the away team mission. The girl drove a brutally hard bargain, but at last, the Ferengi brought together exactly the right combination of tech, promises, Federation technology, and chits. Tivva-ma handed over the minireplicator.

Gleefully, Quark hopped to his feet, stopped to pat the little girl on the head (which indignity she took gracefully), and pranced away, dancing in little circles . . . directly into a solid, massive object that felt like a ship's bulkhead but turned out to be the dreaded Constable Odo's immovable chest.

"Well, well, Quark . . . what have we *here?*" Darting his hand faster than the Ferengi's eye could follow, Odo seized hold of Quark's wrist and twisted his hand palm-side up; Quark clenched his hand into a tight fist around his new acquisition.

Odo hummed happily; maintaining the death grip on Quark's wrist, Odo slowly began to metamorphose his other hand into a nightmarish entrenching tool, with huge, jagged, metal shards instead of fingers. The metal claw snapped open and closed a few times; then it began to move inexorably toward Quark's clenched fist with terrible purpose.

Quark screamed and opened his hand by reflex, as quickly as he would have jerked his fingers from a red-hot hunk of metal. Odo's hand contraption expertly plucked the minireplicator from Quark's trembling paw.

"That's mine!" shouted Quark. "You can't have it!"

"Oh? And how, exactly, did you get it?"

"I bought it legitimately," said the Ferengi stuffily.

"From whom?"

"From Tivva-ma."

"You bought it legitimately by tricking a *child* out of it?"

"I didn't trick her! I paid very handsomely for it."

"And you paid what, exactly, Quark?"

The Ferengi licked his lips, wondering just how much of the truth to tell. "I, uh, gave her a force beam projector and an antigrav device." *Best not tell him about the Tiffnaki death ray,* Quark decided.

Odo arched his eyebrows. "Correct me if I'm wrong, Quark, but didn't those devices belong to the Tiffnakis already?"

"Well . . . I bought them earlier."

"With what?"

"With these." Inspired, Quark dug into his pockets and coughed up another handful of chits.

"You bought *three* devices from credulous Natives with little pieces of paper marked in your *own* handwriting. . . . Is that your story, Quark?" The constable curled his lip.

Quark scowled; as usual, the witless Constable Odo, unable to win a fair battle of the minds, was resorting to sarcasm and mockery. "Well, earlier I traded them some of my glowtubes, and a ph . . ."

"A *fffff*? What's a *fffff*?" Odo tilted his head, almost smirking. "Were you about to say a *phaser*? So in addition to theft and fraud upon a child, you *also* engaged in culture contamination. You've had a busy day, haven't you, Quark?"

"Odo, for profit's sake. I was *teaching* them something about money and the market."

Constable Odo perked up. "Well, perhaps they'd enjoy a lesson about jurisprudence, then. I'll have the chief confiscate the phaser; I have more enjoyable duties regarding *you*."

Turning about, Odo stalked toward the fire where the rest of the away team sat; the constable's hand around Quark's wrist shapeshifted into an iron manacle, and the Ferengi was dragged, willy-nilly, toward disgrace, dishonor, and the probable loss of the single greatest treasure trove ever discovered by any Ferengi since Grand Nagus Zek first realized the potential of the wormhole to the Gamma Quadrant.

This has not been my day, sighed Quark.

The *Defiant* settled at approximately a fifteen degree angle to the seafloor, according to the sensors. Julian Bashir checked once more on his surgery patients; they were all recovering nicely, sleeping soundly with the help of an alpha rhythm inducer. Nurses Marge and Aaastaak monitored the patients carefully; really, there was no reason for Bashir to stay in sickbay.

He took the turbolift to the bridge, but Dax wasn't there. "Computer," he said, "locate Lieutenant Commander Dax." A few minutes later, he knocked on her quarters door.

"Enter," she said glumly, and the door hissed open.

"Jadzia! Why are you sitting here in the dark?"

She rubbed her temples. "A, I'm trying to get rid of this headache, and B, I'm trying to figure out how the hell we're going to contact the away team. There are so many ionized minerals in the water, I can't get a subspace communication out . . . and we can't beam through this stuff, either; the reflection scrambles the beam pattern."

"You have a headache?" asked Bashir, picking up on the one problem where he could at least have some positive impact. He played his tricorder across her skull, probing for the problem. *Hypertensive,* he thought. . . . Perfectly normal, considering the circumstances. "Let me give you a mild analgesic, if you don't mind."

"Will it make me slow and stupid?" She stared at him with hard, dry eyes. "Because I just can't afford that right now."

"I'm not giving you a sedative." Julian smiled,

and Jadzia couldn't suppress a tiny smile herself. He injected it below the skin of her scalp using the hypospray, and she started feeling better after a few moments.

"Here's the predicament," she said, lying back on top of her rack. "We're stuck on the ocean floor at 1,640 meters below the surface. We can't beam through the water, it's too heavily ionized. We can't send a message to the away team, same reason. And we can't rise out of the surface because the four remaining Cardassians in orbit will spot our leaky impulse thrusters, as will the planetary defenses, and the two of them will bomb us into constituent atoms. Any suggestions from the medical staff?"

"Take your vitamins," said Julian. But it was only a pro forma witticism; inside, he was trying to arrange the situation into a logical, coherent pattern so his superior brain could analyze it. Hiding his advanced genetics from his friends was vital, but not more vital than Jadzia's and everyone else's life.

"Obviously there's no logical engineering fix," said the doctor, "or you'd have already thought of it."

"Thank you."

Julian continued, unsure whether she was being sincere or sarcastic. "So what we're looking for is a solution resulting from thinking *sideways.*"

Jadzia rolled onto her side. "All right, think

sideways. With the Cardassians on the surface, I'll bet Benjamin has his hands full . . . and we *must* find a way to communicate with him to find out whether he can hold out long enough for us to run to the fleet and get a couple of escorts—assuming they're not heavily engaged themselves on the Cardassian border."

Bashir completed the thought: "Or whether the captain and the team need immediate extraction, no matter what."

"So how do we exchange pleasantries with Benjamin and the away team?"

Julian sat down in Jadzia's desk chair, putting his chin in his hands to ponder the problem; then, remembering his own analogy, he stretched out on his side on the floor, facing her. He closed his eyes, trying to envision every crazy method of distance communication he had ever read about, from subspace bouncing to the old radio days of ancient Earth, to semaphor, bagpipes, signal fires, two paper cups connected by a string.

He decided to think out loud, hoping to stimulate the brainy Trill. "I've heard that the old sub—what are they called?—submarines used to extend a wire on a float to the surface so they could send and receive message traffic without surfacing."

"Subspace communications require line of sight; they don't bounce around like electromagnetic waves. The team would have to be within a few kilometers of our antenna . . . and they're not."

"All right, then; how about electromagnetic waves? Old-fashioned radio, I mean."

"But how would we *send* to the captain?" objected Jadzia. "He doesn't have a radio receiver to pick up the signal."

"Can't you rebuild a combadge so it receives radio frequency?"

"Of course. But why would he think to *do* it? We didn't arrange anything like this before they left."

Julian Bashir thought long, hard, hot, heavy, cool, sneaky. He envisioned himself and Jadzia somehow rising from the sea as gods or water sprites. He wondered whether they could replicate a bullhorn on a seventeen-hundred-meter pole, raise it up, and *shout* for the captain.

Julian gasped; he half sat—he had it! but *where had the answer gone?*—then it poured back into his consciousness. "Jadzia," he shouted, startling her so that she sat bolt upright; she clutched her head, swearing lustily. . . . Evidently, the headache was not utterly gone.

"You'd better have *something* after shouting me up like that," she declared, making a threatening fist.

"Jadzia, why merely *communicate* with the captain when we can have a face-to-face meeting instead?"

She considered him for a moment, scanning right to left across his prone body, head to boots; she turned to the empty air next to him.

"Deranged," she said to the man who wasn't there. "Totally deranged."

"No, really. If we transport ourselves to the surface, can't we find the captain?"

"Julian," she explained patiently, "I already told you we can't beam through this water."

"Who said anything about beaming? What about using the runabout?"

Jadzia blinked, startled by the suggestion. "I never even thought of that," she admitted. "It's a nice idea, but the pressure would crush the runabout like a paper lantern. It's not built for that."

"What if we pressurized the inside to match the outside?"

Smiling, the commander said, "That would save the runabout, but *we'd* die from oxygen poisoning. . . . At that pressure, the partial pressure of oxygen is enough to be toxic."

"Put a force shield around the runabout, like the ship has?"

Jadzia considered. "That would delay the crushing, but I still think we wouldn't make it to the surface."

"Replicate armor plating for the hull?"

"We'd need the industrial-sized replicators they have at the shipyards. . . . Ours are much too small."

"All right then," said the good doctor, "one last suggestion: we put a force shield around the runabout to delay the crush, *and* we replicate deep-sea scuba diving gear and wear it on the way up; when the runabout is about to blow, we let the seawater in ourselves, stick the regulators in our mouths, and swim the rest of the way."

Dax stared at Julian, her expression utterly unreadable until the doctor realized she was doing the math in her head—she probably didn't even see him. "You know," she said, "this is going to sound crazy . . . but your crazy scheme might just possibly work." She blinked back to the same space-time coordinates occupied by her body. "Give me a couple of hours to run some simulations, and in the meanwhile, can you set up a scuba holosuite program?"

"Yes, I think so. The experimental holosuite is still on board. Why?"

"Because I need the practice. I've never dived below thirty meters in my life."

Julian Bashir bowed his head. "Your wish, as always, is my command, Jadzia."

Captain Sisko deferred any judgment about Quark and his alleged nefarious activities "until such time as we're not in imminent danger of being blown to small bits"; neither Odo nor Quark was happy about the delay, but it was the fastest way to quench the fire. Sisko was far more concerned with supervising the division of his troops, the Tiffnakis, into a semicoherent military organization.

Though they fought frequent wars with their

neighbors—"oh, enemies all around!" repeated the mayor, Asta-ha—the skirmishes, near as Sisko could sort them out, consisted of two ragtag armies standing in lines, facing each other, and activating various pieces of found technology until one side cut and ran. They had no sense of strategy, tactics, supply lines, military hierarchy, reserves, or anything else routine to armies everywhere else in the quadrant.

He consulted with his two most experienced battlefield commanders: Lieutenant Commander Worf and Master Chief Petty Officer O'Brien. "The first step," rumbled the Klingon, truly in his element leading an army against Cardassians, "is to train an elite corps of commandos. They can train the rest of the troops of the village, and even travel to other villages to train the Natives there."

"Worf's right," said the chief, "but there's nothing in any manual I've ever seen telling how to train a people who don't even know how to use a rope. Without all their fancy tech, they're helpless."

Worf took a long, hard look at O'Brien. "I can think of another great people with that same problem."

"You're not on about Risa again, are you, Worf?" The chief sighed in exasperation. "I *told* you, it's totally different. The natives never even—"

"Gentlemen," said the captain, holding out both hands for silence. "I like the idea of training an elite commando unit; both of you, start picking out who you want to be in it. When you start the training, I want to see both the constable and Quark heavily involved . . . *together.*"

While Worf and O'Brien conducted the planet's first military draft, and Quark and Odo continued to try the Ferengi's case before it got so far as a formal complaint, Captain Sisko paced in the darkness, trying to calm his mind and think clearly, logically. He kept coming back to his ill-fated Scouting trip with the Tiffnakis. *Fundamentally,* he told himself, *I had the right idea: put them in a situation where they CAN'T use their tech and force them to start improvising.*

Genetically, the Tiffnakis and their fellow planeteers—the captain had little experience with worlds that were not unified into a single planetary government. . . . What *did* one call them, other than Natives? Genetically, they were exactly the same as they were when they *created* all that fancy technology; they were obviously intelligent enough to improvise real solutions to their problems. *If only their culture weren't so blasted fixated on techno manna falling from Heaven.*

According to Asta-ha, every one of their rites of passage, at every stage of life, followed the same pattern: put the candidate into a difficult, or at older ages dangerous, situtation, surrounded by various disguised pieces of old tech and new tech; then stand back and wait for the candidate to discover the right piece and use it to solve the problem. But wasn't that in essence the way all science worked? "Finding a smoother pebble or a prettier shell than ordinary, whilst the great ocean of truth lay all undiscovered before me," as Isaac Newton wrote more than six centuries before.

Without realizing it, the Natives might have prepared themselves for their true renascence, as they were ripped from their womb of sleep and thrust into the adult world once again. Sisko chuckled, amazed at his own melodramatic nature; he felt like Captain Ahab, not Captain Sisko, standing one-legged on the deck of the *Pequod,* spouting jeremiads at the great white whale.

But fundamentally, I was RIGHT. He clung to that thought like a shipwrecked sailor to a floating spar. "I just didn't go far enough," he said aloud.

"Beg pardon, sir?" said O'Brien from directly behind the captain.

Suppressing the urge to spin about, Sisko kept his back to the chief, contemplating the horizon. "Fundamentally, I was right," he said, "on the idea of the Scouting trip. I just didn't go far enough. . . . I should have strip-searched the damned Natives before we set out."

Sisko turned; the chief was uncharacteristically silent for a moment before speaking. "I'm, ah, not sure what Keiko would think about me strip-searching females, sir."

The captain snorted. "I think we can trust the

women to search the women and the men to search the men; I don't think we should be involved at all. But we *must* impress upon them the urgency of keeping *nothing* technological. Nothing."

"Um, how about rope, sir?"

"No. Nothing but their clothes . . . and run a tricorder over the clothing to make sure there's nothing hidden. We'll *teach* them how to weave rope."

"Food?"

"We'll pick it, pluck it, or catch it."

"All right. Does that apply to the instructors as well?" Sisko chuckled. *Not unless we have a death wish,* he thought. "Aye, aye, sir," said O'Brien. "Then what? Where are we going?"

"The commandos, led by the away team, are going to watch the Cardassians conquer another village. I want Asta-ha and her raiders to see how an enemy strikes—and how their own people fall apart when their little toys are taken away."

"I . . . don't know that I could just stand my ground and watch women and kids being killed, Captain."

Sisko felt his own gut tighten, but he had long ago learned the primary Law of Command: sometimes, you simply have to let some people die to save a larger or more important group. "You won't have to, Chief. But these people, they're asleep. We have to shock them to wake them up, and this is the only way to do it."

O'Brien turned to stare at the same horizon that the captain had found so fascinating a few moments before; was he seeing the same visions, or his own, private, Boschian hell? "Aye, aye, Cap'n. I'll tell Worf."

"Muster the troops and the away team in one hour and we'll begin stripping away their manna."

CHAPTER
13

NEVER, in more than twenty years of hard service in Starfleet, training scores—hundreds—of young enlisted men and even a few officers, *never* had Chief Miles Edward O'Brien had to nanny such a whiny group of complainers as were these Natives. Everything was all wrong. The hike was too long; the slope was too steep; the ground was too hard; the sun was too hot; the wind was too windy; the rocks were too rocky. By the time the nonchalant Captain Sisko had led them but thirteen kilometers "into the wild," Chief O'Brien was wishing he had palmed one of those force beam projectors to whack a few of his squad members over the head.

"Sure," grumbled the chief to Worf, "what does *he* care about all the complaining?" He nodded his head at the captain, as if Worf might not understand who *he* was. "He doesn't have to hear it. He's up there at the front, gawking at blue trees and birds with metallic feathers. . . . *We're* the ones back here having to stomach all this junk."

Worf growled deep in his throat. "Chief O'Brien, you are making as much noise as they." Miles raised his eyebrows; whenever Worf resorted to calling him *Chief O'Brien,* it meant the huge Klingon was at the end of his rope. "Can you not just be silent except when correction is called for?" Suddenly, Worf pointed at Owena-da, who had stopped by the side of the road and was staring at the ground as if looking for something. "You! Get back in line—"

Owena-da looked back at Worf, blinking in confusion. "Neg, fellow—I mean, no sir, I thought I saw the sparkle of new tech among the weeds here. In fact . . ."

Owena-da reached for a small box, the size of a tricorder, but Worf was quicker. He flashed past Chief O'Brien before the latter even registered what Owena-da was doing, and tramped down on the "new tech" with Federation-standard footgear that somehow looked more like an iron-shod jackboot when Worf wore it. "I see no new tech," said the Klingon.

"It's right there, under your foot."

Worf crouched down to look the frightened Tiffnaki in the eyes. "I see no new tech," he repeated, his voice taking on an unmistakable tone of menace.

Owena-da swallowed hard. "You're, ah, right; I must've been mistaken, sir. There's no new tech beneath your boot."

"Get—in—*LINE!*"

The Tiffnaki didn't waste any time; he shot past O'Brien faster even than Worf had, but in the other direction. By the time the chief swiveled his head, Owena-da was back at his assigned row and file, matching steps with the other Tiffnakis in the march. "Well," remarked O'Brien to his friend when the Klingon returned, "I suppose that's one way of stopping them from whining. Now are you going to scare the rest of them half to death?"

Worf shot O'Brien a look, and the chief grinned. He allowed his stride to shorten as he moved outside, and the column marched past him; when he was even with Odo and Quark, the rear guards, O'Brien tried his complaint again, this time to more receptive ears.

"I know exactly what you mean," sympathized Quark, shooting a venomous sideways glance at the constable. "Being around people who spend all day, every day complaining about this or that tiny little infraction of the most insignificant regulation, makes me want to pack it all up and move somewhere."

"Oh, really, Quark?" said Odo, his lip curling. "Well, who's stopping you?"

"You know," mused the Ferengi, "maybe it is time I made some lifestyle changes. All that hustle and bustle on the station—Quark, fetch me another drink. Quark, the Rigelian bloodwine is too cold. Quark, the *gagh* is too sluggish!"

"Oh, my heart just bleeds for you; *when* did you say you were leaving?"

"And the help!" Quark smacked his forehead and stared skyward, as if appealing to the Final Accountant. "Rom was bad enough, but those Bajorans that Kai Winn brought over with her. You'd think their Prophets had something *against* alcohol, synthehol, and Dabo girls."

"Why, I can't imagine what."

Quark and Odo were on such a roll that O'Brien felt himself jollied right out of his mood just listening to the pair.

"So I thought that maybe . . ." Quark leaned close to O'Brien to speak in a conspiratorial whisper; Constable Odo made no effort to move closer, but the chief noticed that Odo's ears grew distinctly larger. *The advantages of a shapeshifting eavesdropper,* thought O'Brien. "Perhaps," continued Quark, "the captain wouldn't be averse to my moving to some nice, quiet, out-of-the-way planet more or less permanently."

"Such as here," suggested O'Brien.

Quark shrugged. "If you like. Someplace where I could settle down, grow some roots—"

"Mine a little latinum," added the constable without missing a beat.

"And so what if I do? Is there some *law* against honest labor, a day's pay for a good day's toil?"

"If there is, Quark," smirked Odo, "that's probably the only law you're in no danger of breaking."

Before Quark could respond to the latest outrage, a whisper traveled along the column: "Silence behind—on the signal, break ranks, find cover in the woods."

O'Brien watched Captain Sisko, way at the front of the regiment-sized column; without further warning, the captain raised his left hand flat and touched his right fist to the left palm, the signal for "Attention." Then he gestured to the right with his now-opened right hand. . . . "Scatter; cover," the signal meant.

O'Brien raced for the silver blue woods, leaping over a thicket of purple berry plants; this time, most of the regiment actually beat him to the tree line, though it still took them too long to fall flat behind something solid. Sisko waited in front of the trees until he could see no one; then he melded into the forest himself and vanished. Even knowing where the captain was, O'Brien could barely pick him out from among the trunks, now bluish gray in the waning sunlight, under the first moon. Even Odo awkwardly hid behind a tree, though the chief could tell he would have been happier *becoming* a tree.

Chief O'Brien listened closely but heard only the faintest of rustlings as somebody squirmed to a more comfortable position. *At least no one shushed him this time,* laughed the chief silently to himself.

The last time, the chorus of shushes were so loud, they totally drowned out the squirming unfortunate.

O'Brien heard the tramping of boots. From around a bend ahead of them came a troop of Natives. . . . *Probably enemies of the Tiffnakis,* thought the chief nervously; he had not forgotten Asta-ha's insistance that "enemies are all around." They were, on the whole, taller than the Tiffnakis, and all had silvery hair. *Either it's a dye job,* thought O'Brien, *or there's REALLY no interbreeding between the villages.* They all dressed similarly in togalike wrapping garments, unlike the Tiffnakis, who dressed like a roomful of color-blind Ferengis, grabbing jackets and pantaloons at random from a bin, no two alike.

The ghostly parade shuffled silently down the road; they sported a guidon carrying a guidon: a white, triangular pennant that flapped in the breeze, seemingly glued to a curved, sectioned pole that looked as if it would expand and contract like a pointer. Glancing neither left nor right, the fifty or so Natives marched on past.

O'Brien held his breath; the last encounter had not gone well. Despite nearly a whole day working with the Tiffnakis on the principle of *concealment*—"such a powerful new tech that requires no device . . . better even than rope tech," insisted Asta-ha—they had made so much noise, each person trying to shuffle to a more comfy position or better concealment, or loudly shushing the other noisemakers, that the previous troop the Tiffnakis passed had easily heard them.

That group, who looked like a contingent of Highland Scots with kilts and feathered blouses, had stopped and stared at the hedgerow behind which the Tiffnakis attempted to conceal themselves; then one of them pointed a device at the semihidden mob, and the hedges flattened like they'd been blown over by gale-force winds. O'Brien had felt the push from the probing force beam, but he refused to react; alas, the Tiffnakis evidently decided the game was up, and they *stood up,* waving to the kilt wearers, who turned out to be friends of theirs (one of the few other Natives who weren't Tiffnaki enemies, again according to Astaha—who evidently thought her hereditary position largely required keeping lists of who around them was naughty and nice).

It was a fiasco, of course; it took Worf and O'Brien fully fifteen minutes to restore some sense of order and get the two mobs of friendly Natives separated again. Quark and Odo were no help whatsoever, especially after Quark accused Odo of shapeshifting, a direct violation of the captain's orders; the ensuing argument, pursued in loud whispers to keep it from the ears of the curious Tiffnakis, occupied both the constable and the Ferengi. Captain Sisko ignored the scene, observing the ruddy sun sinking toward the horizon. The chief had to admit the sky turned a beautiful shade of amber, then purple, then dark blue, due to the metallic dust in the atmosphere; the Whatsit planet boasted three moons, but only two were visible from the surface. . . . The two shining together cast about half the light of Earth's gigantic moon, Luna. But annoyed as the chief was, he knew that Sisko was only exercising the CO's prerogative of leaving all the headaches to his XO . . . Lieutenant Commander Worf, in this case.

As the new group passed by, Chief O'Brien tried to lick his lips with a tongue as dry as the dust he lay in; the silent phantoms scuffed along the trail, holding some wicked-looking devices at port arms. From the hang and the care the women took with them—only the women carried the devices—the chief knew they were hefty weapons of unknown technology . . . and on Sierra-Bravo 112-II, *unknown technology* was a deadly term.

He turned his head slowly to the left, careful not to make any moves sudden enough to catch a glance, or to rustle any leaves. Owena-da was nearby, and from the tension with which the weapon master of the Tiffnakis clenched his fists and his jaw, O'Brien knew these Natives were no friends of the Tiffnakis.

Abruptly, everything was *real;* this was no longer a Scouting hike into the Big Woods; the exercise fell into focus for what it was: a military excursion into enemy territory, where a single dumb mistake could cost people their lives. Possibly even members of the away team.

The chief had only one hole card; he had held back a small hand phaser, concealed in his boot, when the captain ordered everyone stripped. "He only means the men," insisted the chief to Worf, nodding at the Tiffnakis, but he didn't check with the captain, not wanting to find out he was wrong. Worf seemed skeptical; but O'Brien would bet his last replicator ration that the Klingon had not completely disarmed himself, either.

O'Brien watched the toga-wearing Natives shuffle past . . . and realized to his amazement that they hadn't noticed a thing. In only the second test of the Tiffnaki ability to grasp the brand-new concept of *hiding,* they looked to have scored a bull's-eye.

He felt like half a man as Sisko resumed the march; but he wasn't too self-absorbed to notice that time and patience had proved the captain right. the Tiffnakis, hence Natives in general, were trainable. The war for Sierra-Bravo 112-II no longer looked quite so bleak.

After several hours of annoying bandying with the Ferengi bartender, Odo reached his limit of tolerance. He knew the next stupid insult, the next clumsy attempt to stake a claim on the topsoil of the planet, even the next arrogant sneer directed at anyone motivated by any principle loftier than profit, and orders or no, Odo would change his fist into a sledgehammer and pound Quark right into the ground he so coveted. To spare everyone the pain and heartache, the constable turned about and strode into the blackness of night.

Seeing was no problem; away from prying eyes, he risked a little bit of shapeshifting to give himself owl eyes. . . . In fact, he had been working on the entire bird, but the eye-morph was as far as he was willing to push the captain's strict prohibition. Odo stared around the bleak landscape, realizing that anyone with infrared sensors or light-amp goggles could see the Tiffnakis as plainly as if the sun were up. *Well, Captain Sisko has the tricorder, and he's convinced we're alone out here.* Of course, if one of the Natives—ridiculous name, so typical of Commander Dax—if one of the Natives had a sensor shield, the regiment could be in for a rude shock.

He stared up at the sky, feeling a terrible sense of lonliness and—anxiety. Something was dreadfully wrong with the scenario, but Odo simply couldn't put his fist on it.

Without even noticing, he found his feet directed him toward the captain's circle of firelight as if they had a mind of their own. *Well, technically they do, I guess,* he realized; Founders—changelings—didn't have a distinct central nervous system or brain, of course, else they could never transform into anything flat; the Founders' mental activity occurred everywhere and nowhere . . . which only meant that the language of "solids"—terrible term— simply wasn't equipped to handle the biomorphogenic concepts.

"Good evening, Odo," said the captain without turning around. "Sit down, take a load off your mind."

Had Odo been the gasping sort, this would have been a good time: how did Captain Sisko always seem to know what he was thinking? "I've been thinking about the *Defiant,*" he said, nervous at the lie. "I'm very concerned about Commander Dax and our transportation back home."

"As are we all, Odo." Odo's eyes were good enough to see the captain's tense jaw and shoulder muscles. *Yes, you especially must be frantic,* thought the constable.

"Even if we win this war, and I'm not admitting the probability yet, how would we even let anyone know we're here?"

Captain Sisko smiled mysteriously. "Actually, I've been playing with one or two of the toys we removed from our pack rat troops," he said, "and I'm more than ever convinced that their ancestors *did* have warp field technology."

"They did? You're sure about that, Captain?"

"Some of these components look so damned familiar, but just different enough. Given a few months, I'm sure that Chief O'Brien and I could build a workable subspace communicator powerful enough to reach to the nearest Federation outpost."

Odo frowned, wishing he could imitate more subtle emotions. "If they had warp technology, then why didn't they leave the planet?"

"Maybe they did, Odo." The captain gestured Odo toward the fire, perhaps forgetting that a changeling didn't get cold. Quickly morphing his eyes back to normal, the constable sat where he was directed.

"You think they did leave this planet, sir? Could you elaborate?"

The captain shrugged. "There are simply too few, ah, Natives for a technology this advanced. The traces of warp technology, the advanced tech—more advanced in many ways than ours—make me suspicious. How can a culture develop antigravity, force beams, and all those other things and *not* develop warp drive?"

"So . . . they were here and they left? But where? Why?"

"Who can say? The first thing I would check is whether the Natives and all the other plant and animal life here share the same DNA; this might have been a forgotten colony."

"I believe Dax did so; they evolved here."

"In any event, for some reason, the ancestors of the Natives stripped all warp technology from the planet before they left: they wanted these people to stay."

Odo had a disturbing thought; he mulled it over for a moment, then offered it. "Captain, could this planet have been a penal colony or medical-quarantine planet? Or a—what did your planet use to call it?—a lunatic asylum?"

"Unless we locate central records of some sort,

we'll never know." Captain Sisko leaned forward to milk the fire of all the heat he could. "Well, unless we can help these people throw out the Cardassians and the Drek'la, it's going to become a *slave* colony, just like Bajor was."

Odo heard the crunch of hurrying footsteps long before the captain, with merely solid ears, could do so. "Sounds like Commander Worf is on his way here, double time," he warned.

Captain Sisko stood to receive his executive officer.

Worf spoke quickly in a low tone, not to be overheard. Of course, Odo heard perfectly: "Captain, tricorder readings of fuel cell emissions indicate the Cardassians are on the move again. Asta-ha believes they are headed toward a city of people called Druvats-nasas that is only fifteen kilometers away. If we hurry, we can reach a bluff that overlooks the city before the Cardassians arrive in force."

The captain nodded. "Rouse the troops for a night march, Commander; get them moving in ten minutes."

"Aye, aye, sir," said the Klingon with a vengeful grin that made the constable shudder.

CHAPTER
14

ODO FELT very uncomfortable with the military turn of events, aware he knew absolutely nothing about military discipline and strategy. His only duty, he decided, was to obey orders and to keep Quark in line: the creeping Ferengi had already tried to sabotage the development of the planetary natives once by corrupting them with the concepts of money, capitalism, and profit, before they were ready to develop them on their own; and Quark had also made several serious attempts (worthy of formal charges upon return to the station) to exploit the planetary resources without authorization from the planetary ruling body.

But what IS the planetary ruling body? wondered the constable. He had never before dealt with a situation of such anarchy, where there was no world government. *How can anybody ever decide to do anything. . . . Who supplies the authority to—to build a village, dam a river, or even plough a field?* After all, virtually anything one could do would affect people all around. . . . Plough a field and you change the local ecosystem for your neighbors, driving away roaming animals and attracting insectal (and insectivorous) pests. Irrigation would alter the water table; even the very air could be affected.

As the unruly mob of Tiffnakis were whipped into a semblance of order by Commander Worf with his bellows and Chief O'Brien with angry gestures and "butt-chewing" (a solid term Odo found distasteful in the extreme), the constable threw his entire energies into rousing the practically somnambulant Quark and prodding him into shouldering his pack and falling in at the rear of the column. Still he fretted: how was it possible for an individual Tiffnaki to make even the simplest decision without a single controlling legal authority to set the rules? Odo shook his head; it was yet another mystery of solids . . . *worth a long conversation with Nerys—with Major Kira—when I get back.*

Something else nagged at the constable. It had been nearly fourteen hours since he had last been able to slip away during the night and revert to liquid form, and now they were headed out on a march that surely would take Odo "past his bedtime," as Commander Dax would probably put it.

Feeling apprehension, Constable Odo scanned the bleak surrounding countryside for someplace to hide; he found nothing.

But then, sentient solids generally had very poor night vision, sacrificed in evolution's blind drive toward the larger brain. The darkness itself was Odo's friend.

Still, he needed that controlling legal authority. Leaving the half-asleep Quark, Odo hurried his pace and caught up with the captain just as the latter gave the order to "head 'em up and move 'em out."

"Sir, may I speak to you privately?"

"Certainly, Odo. I'm always happy to talk to you."

"Captain, it's getting to be about that time."

"Time?"

"For me to regenerate."

Captain Sisko raised his eyebrows; he often forgot the needs of his shapechanging constable, especially after Odo's lengthy interregnum as a solid himself. "Odo, I cannot possibly delay the march."

"No, and I wouldn't ask you. All I ask . . ." Odo simulated a deep breath, a habit he had picked up during the interregnum; strangely, it still worked to calm him down and center him. "All I ask," he said quietly, "is for you to leave me behind; let me liquefy for a few hours. . . . Then when I'm myself again, let me shapechange to a hawk and rejoin you."

188

The captain frowned. "I'm reluctant to allow you to do any shapechanging here. We've already pushed the limit of the Prime Directive."

"I won't let anyone see me if I can help it. I'll add a bluish tint to my feathers, and perhaps I'll be mistaken for a local avian even if I am spotted."

Captain Sisko struggled with his first inclination for a moment, then relaxed. "All right, Constable; Worf will show you where we're headed and give you the approximate time of arrival; but *I want you there* when the battle commences. I need your eyes, Odo."

"I'll be there," the constable promised.

He consulted Worf, then left the outraged Chief O'Brien in charge of Quark. Then Odo let himself slip farther and farther behind the march as "rear guard," finally stopping, shapechanging into a hawk for practice, and flying far enough aside that even a sharp-eyed Klingon shouldn't be able to see him in the one-mooned gloom. He found a vaguely cup-shaped indentation in a rock; with a deep sigh of relaxation, Odo squatted in it and allowed his form to break down into the sensuous, liquid pool.

He slept and he dreamed, something unusual: Odo remembered his brief interlude in the memory pool of the Founders, on his homeworld, the embracing peace of being part of the whole, in his proper order, surrounded by and filled with his own kind. Odo dreamed of touching minds, being At One—a concept frequently enunciated but never truly understood by any solid creature, forever locked away from its fellows by walls of flesh and bone.

When he jerked awake, many hours later, at first he couldn't remember which "one" he was supposed to be. It was a delicious feeling at first; then he remembered he was supposed to do something, something urgent—and he panicked until, by force of habit, he rose as Constable Odo again. The task jumped back into his consciousness.

Settle, settle, he commanded himself to little avail. The horizon was lightening; it was later than he planned.

It was *three forty-one.* Odo was shocked to discover he had *overslept.* Nervously, he tapped the combadge: "Odo to Captain Sisko." No reply, so he tried again.

Odo was stumped. No response from the *Defiant* he could understand: they had left orbit. But until this moment, the combadges had been working person to person among the away team. Something (or someone) was jamming the signal. . . . *Well, if it's the Cardassians, I'd better get aloft.*

Furious at himself, and dreading the captain's animadversions almost more than the possibility of mission failure, Odo burst into the form of the hawk again and flapped aloft, only remembering the color-tinting minutes later.

Once at cruising altitude, carrying the combadge safely tucked inside his abdomenal cavity, the constable was surprised anew, as he was every time, at the freedom he felt from earthly restraint.

He soared, feeling almost as if he could flap harder and harder and fly right into orbit. He circled for a few moments, finding his bearings; Odo had to compare the two-dimensional line rendering of the terrain with its topographic symbols and contour lines to the living, pulsing, three-dimensional, full-color image hawk eyes sent to hawk brain.

At half a kilometer in altitude, the sun had already dawned, though it wasn't yet five o'clock local time; remembering the tilt and rotation of the planet, Odo oriented himself the correct direction, and of a sudden, the map and the territory merged and he saw his route. He pushed his head and neck forward and pumped powerful wings to eat up the kilometers. Odo saw no Cardassian vehicles along the route; evidently, they were not the ones jamming the combadge's subspace transmission. *Could there be some sort of planetwide defenses?* mused the constable. Surely Cardassians had no subspace countermeasures strong enough to jam a combadge from orbit.

Even as the hawk flies, fifteen kilometers is no negligible distance; by the time Odo could see the lights of the city, and the bluffs overlooking them—filled, as he squinted his eyes, with creeping, spreading Tiffnakis and the away team—the terminator line, with the brightness of daylight right behind, was already crawling across the city of the Druvats-nasas and headed toward Captain Sisko's regiment at their position in the heights. Odo couldn't help being astonished at the blue gray beauty of Sierra-Bravo 112-II in dawn's light: the high metal content highlighted every color with shimmers and sparkles, while the dust in the atmosphere drew out the reds and yellows of the sun, forming an inverse of the holosuite program of Earth's Bryce Canyon. . . . On Sierra-Bravo, it was the iron-latinum cliffs that were Magritte blue and the sky that was rust red.

From his height, Odo saw another sight to freeze him solid: an advancing line of Cardassian planet-skimmers headed toward the town, then pulled up short, freezing in place . . . except for one, solitary skimmer that set out at an oblique angle for the captain's position.

At first, the hawk's spirit leapt; they were discovered. Then the Cardassian stopped, and Odo realized the true destination: a small, rounded building that resembled an oversized mushroom cap. The Cardassian in the single skimmer fired his disruptor at the building, evidently blowing the lock; then he stepped inside.

An instant later, the lights of Druvats-nasas town flashed bright and faded instantly, and the constable understood. The rest of the column resumed its drive; the attack was underway.

For a moment, Odo hesitated, making long, lazy circles in the air, catching the hot, rising currents off the already day-lit bluffs. *What is my duty here? Must I rejoin the captain immediately, or should I act as his eyes?* From the regiment's vantage point, they couldn't have seen the Cardassian skim to the powerhouse and cut off the broadcast power—so in a sense, Odo's tardiness already had paid a dividend.

Well, that's one way to rationalize it, he thought bitterly; it sounded just like one of Quark's post hoc "explanations." Regardless, however, the constable continued to circle above the battle, alternating between using his hawk eyes to view individual actions with telescopic precision or pulling back to more normal eyes to view the larger picture.

The battle was as devastating as the one in the Tiffnaki village: without the power broadcast to animate the tech they had come to depend upon, the Druvats-nasas were helpless before the onslaught. The invaders used no particular finesse or grand strategy; after cutting the local power relay, they simply disembarked from their skimmers and walked forward in a straight line, sweeping disruptors back and forth across the defenseless mob.

There was of course nothing the Druvats-nasas could do; there was nothing that Commander Dax could have done—and Odo made a mental note to tell her that, next time he saw her. *IF I see her again,* he added with a chill. With the *Defiant* missing in action and Dax nonresponsive on the nonexistent subspace comm link, it was beginning to look doubtful that Odo would see anything familiar again. . . . Not even his wonderful, old bucket, or the bucket-of-bolts station that contained it.

The villagers fell back, more orderly at first than

the Tiffnakis had been; but it made no difference in the long run—when the Druvats-nasas line broke, it broke suddenly, like a dam collapsing outward from a single crack at the center. Watching as a hawk, Odo had already picked out the obvious leader of the village, the hereditary mayor, or whatever they called the post; he was a man with immensely long, reddish blue hair hanging across his naked torso to his waist, where he had tucked it into a green sash he wore. A powerful man with corded neck muscles reminding Odo of a bull's, and supplying the constable with ideas for future shapeshifting experiments.

When the leader suddenly threw down his useless rifle and bolted for the rear of the central company of defenders, his nearest comrades-at-arms panicked first; the rout spread from the center out, as more and more Druvats-nasas realized the futility of their position, and then saw their own leader running like a thief in the night. The one-sided firefight was over in nine minutes.

The line comprised no more than twenty Drek'la and the two commanding Cardassians, but they overran the village and seized the four core buildings, which outlined a large village green (or village blue, actually) filled with booths. Odo swept a little closer and saw that the booths contained grab bags full of tech; at the back of each booth were a number of targets and trinkets for testing the new toys as people acquired them. The Drek'la began burning the targets with their disruptors, for no other reason that Odo could see but sheer devilry.

The other Cardassian, the one who cut the power, rejoined his compatriots. He climbed out of his skimmer with little of the usual Cardassian strut; he stood, hands clasped behind his back, viewing the pillaging.

Something struck Constable Odo about the man, something wrong and out of place; but he couldn't quite put his talon on it. He continued to circle, to watch, knowing his instinct was trying to tell him something—but not yet what it was. *I'd better have something worthwhile for the captain, considering how angry he's going to be anyway.*

The Cardassian observed for a while; then he slipped into a shadowy recess to gather some of the devices that had fallen over when other invaders destroyed the stall. At once, the incongruity struck Odo full force: Cardassians were arrogant, strutting, condescending figures, each of whom thought himself more than the equal of all the other Cardassians; they thought of themselves as the elder race, civilized long before most of the others, and they observed the "young" races much as one would observe a monkey or a Thoractian curltail. . . . But this one was turning the same clinical gaze on the Drek'la—*and the other Cardassian.*

There was no trace of the swagger of Gul Dukat in the lone Cardassian's stride; there wasn't even the overly self-effacing preening of Garak, back on the station. There was the cold, clinical gaze of a zookeeper.

While he watched, circling around and around, Odo *thought* he saw something else. In reaching for one of the fallen pieces of tech, Odo could almost have sworn that he saw the Cardassian's arm lengthen to the ground, grab the gun, then return to its normal length.

He was so stunned, he almost forgot how to fly. *Founders? A* Founder *is with the invaders?* He thought for a moment, turning his loops into figure eights. *Or perhaps,* he admitted, *a Founder is* leading *the invaders.*

Then the questionable soldier looked up, fixing Odo with a piercing glare of his own. Feeling suddenly terribly vulnerable himself, Odo decided on a bold approach: he picked from the air a spot where many Druvats-nasas defenders had died. Swooping down on the spot, Odo walked behind a body, flaring his wings, and pecked at the ground behind the corpse. Odo fervently hoped that the Cardassian, whether Founder or not, would be fooled by the perspective into thinking that the hawk was actually eating the dead flesh.

It seemed to work; when Odo looked up a moment later, the lone Cardassian was gone. But the constable was shaken. *I don't know for sure what I saw,* he told himself, *but it's hard to deceive the eyes I'm currently wearing.*

Odo continued pretending to peck at dead bodies, waiting for an opportunity to lift off and return to Captain Sisko's vista point. At least now, Constable Odo reflected, he certainly had enough new intelligence that the captain would probably forgive him the minor indiscretion of oversleeping his watch.

As it happened, Chief O'Brien was the first to spot the spectral hawk circling far above the carnage. "Commander," he said, nudging the Klingon and pointing at the bird.

"What about it?" answered Worf in an irritated voice.

"Five days of replicator rations says it's Odo, spying for us."

"Hm," said Worf; then he said it again and rose to crawl toward the captain.

O'Brien continued to watch the hawk, seeing it circle, circle: the prodigal bird returned, and lo, it *was* Constable Odo. He stood tall, a tempting target were he not far enough back from the edge of the cliff to avoid detection. O'Brien saw Worf and the captain slithering toward Odo, and he quickly joined them; Quark, meanwhile, had also noticed Odo but was moving *away* from his ancient foe.

"I think I saw something," said the constable gravely. "If so, it's grave news indeed, Captain."

"What is it?" asked Sisko, in a voice indicating he really didn't need any more grave surprises.

"I think one of the Cardassians isn't a Cardassian," said the constable. "Captain . . . I believe at least one of the Cardassian overseers leading the Drek'la is a Founder. And the other Cardassians don't know it."

It was Worf who made the intuitive leap: "If that is true, Captain, then I believe we are dealing with a renegade contingent of Cardassians. If they were with the main force, the Founder would not be hiding his presence from the rest of them."

"My God, Worf," said O'Brien, "you've hit it on the head. These aren't Cardassian invaders. . . . They're Cardassian *fugitives.*"

CHAPTER
15

AT THE darkest crystal of night, when the world is at its stillest, comes first the faint tinkle of morning, heralding the light that will shatter the blackness like hammer against glass. Captain Benjamin Sisko lay at the top of the bluff, staring down at the smouldering ruins of the Druvats-nasas village, raked by disruptor fire in a profligate waste of life and property; and when did Cardassians ever care for another's life, somebody else's property?

But spread to either side of the captain, his own Tiffnaki commandos radiated their own burning light of revenge and anger. When their own village was destroyed, they were too demoralized, frightened, ashamed, and stunned to nurse the feelings of injustice and rage necessary to spark a rebellion against overwhelming odds: *Fiat justitia, ruat caelum*—Let justice be done, though heaven fall.

Perspective, thought Sisko, *that's what's needed.* It was not the slaves directly under the whip who rebelled against early Earth slavery; it was a slave who had escaped slavery, Frederick Douglass, who was the movement's most gifted orator. *And closer to home,* he thought, *the Cardassians were driven off Bajor not by those who were most directly controlled, such as Kai Winn, but by the freedom fighters in Shakar's and other groups who had momentarily escaped the lash.* Perspective: his Tiffnakis needed the perspective of seeing the pain, blood, and humiliation of other Natives to awaken the burning flames of justice in themselves. . . . And that was no distorted reflection on them; it was a universal truth.

Benjamin Sisko looked left and right; the Cardassians had long since won, and there was little reason to fear they would scan the overlooking cliffs for observers. But the Tiffnaki commandos were silent with hatred and bitter resolve, to a man and woman of them. The flesh of the once chipper, voluble Asta-ha was pale blue, and Owena-da clenched his fists so hard, Sisko heard the bones crack from three meters away.

Sisko knew what the scene would look like back at the main encampment, where they had left the rest of the villagers, once they had all been told the evidence that only a handful had seen this day: the men would stop chattering, the women would dress for camouflage. Both would begin finding metal (in abundance on Sierra-Bravo), crystal, anything that would take an edge. Even the little children left behind at the river, even Tivva-ma, would take to crying silently—not with a wail, as a child wanting attention uses (how well he remembered Jake as a child), but simply letting the tears roll unheeded down their grimy cheeks, neither demanding nor even expecting a grown-up to do anything about their pain.

Captain Sisko had seen wars; he had seen war with the Cardassians. He even remembered himself, if it really was himself, in the years just after the Borg killed Jennifer, his wife and Jake's mother. *I've set them on the road to a terrible future,* he thought in leaden silence, *but what else could I do? We MUST believe that death is better than subjugation and slavery—or why would anyone EVER resist the tyrant?*

With a gesture, Sisko drew his freedom fighters back from the brink. They crawled slowly backwards until the village was no longer visible—hence they were no longer visible to the Druvatsnasas village. Then they stood, and flanked by the reassembled away team, they beat a cold, quiet retreat. Nobody spoke but Asta-ha, hereditary mayor, and all she said was, "We will learn the new tech, Sisko; neg, we are not fools." She said it as if Sisko had implied they were.

Well, perhaps I did, thought the captain sadly; he'd tried not to let his annoyance and disappointment show, but it probably came across despite best intentions. Sisko felt a gigantic presence loom behind him and heard the crunch of boots that had never even attempted to sneak quietly. "Commander Worf," he acknowledged without turning around.

"Captain, what is the destination of our march?"

Wordlessly, Sisko turned and walked at a right angle to the rest of the troop, followed by the Klingon; when Asta-ha looked questioningly at him, he said, "Carry on, Mayor." The Tiffnakis continued their slow, beaten march.

"Worf," said the captain quietly, "we must rejoin the main force. I suspect you will see a gratifying seriousness of purpose among the commandos now."

The Klingon curled his lip. "Then they *were* tweaking our beards. I knew they must have been. . . . Nobody is so witless as to think it perfectly fine to—"

"Commander," said the captain, so low that Worf had to pause and cock his ear to hear, "they were born into a culture where 'found tech' was the only way they had to solve problems. Don't be too harsh." Sisko smiled faintly and whispered, *"Who but a Klingon could follow Kahless?"* in Worf's native tongue.

The Klingon calmed down, breathing slower and deeper, and the captain continued. "We've turned them, Worf; they finally understand the stakes. Let's wait and see what happens over the next few days, on the way back." Captain Sisko grinned like a grim Ferengi: "I've mapped out another Scouting trail for the return trip."

How on God's blue Sierra-Bravo does he expect to do anything with this lot? Chief O'Brien sighed; nothing that Captain Sisko had done should have had any effect whatsoever. And when the column came to another cliff, and Sisko ordered yet another rappelling "evolution," O'Brien expected exactly the same shenanigans as the last time.

But something seemed to have seeped into their heads. Something! O'Brien set the phasing stakes, grunted the anchors into place, and hurled the ropes over the edge. One didn't clear the base of the cliff, snarling on a teal scrub line with branches shaped just like grappling hooks; the chief labored to haul it back up again for another cast.

"You know, Worf," he said, "there's a wide difference between the officer who says, 'set those anchors,' and the working man who has to sweat them into place."

The Klingon, who had been studiously ignoring the drama with the rope, turned a scowling face toward O'Brien. "If you are incapable of casting the line far enough, I will do it for you."

"I can throw a damned line! I was just commenting on . . ." O'Brien returned to his task, grumbling. It wasn't that setting the lines was particularly heavy labor. *It's the sheer futility of it all!* O'Brien was already fuming that after all this work, the Tiffnakis were just going to make a mockery of it again.

But when the lines were properly set, and the Natives began to rappel down the cliff, the chief's mouth dropped and stayed open until the first wave hit the ground. The Tiffnakis carried out the entire evolution exactly as taught at Starfleet Academy.

No cheating. No magic. No teleportation or flying carpets or pocket elevators. Mayor General Asta-ha dropped in the first wave; she squirmed into a harness, hooked her carabiner into the line, and stepped backwards over the edge. The carabiners, being safety equipment, were among the only pieces of technology that the captain had allowed the Tiffnakis from the well-stocked backpacks the away team still carried from the first Scouting trip.

The chief winced a bit, watching her make that first step into thin, thin air, suspended only by a string, dangling a hundred meters above the ground. But Asta-ha seemed not even to *notice* the drop beneath her feet. *It's like she never developed the normal fear of falling,* he decided, *since the damned "new tech" has always been there to save her.* The rest of the Tiffnaki commandos followed three by three, each showing the same lack of fear about the height as their mayor general.

Drukulu-da, the "historian" of the mob, if O'Brien's universal translator was doing its job, got into trouble going down the cliff; he let himself go too fast, burned his hands, and in a panic, yanked himself to a halt halfway down the cliff face. When Worf shouted for Drukulu-da to continue, the historian yelled back that the rope had slipped along the carabiner and was trapped against the "Swiss seat" harness he sat in.

Drukulu-da had only made the commando cut at the last minute when another Tiffnaki was eliminated making a rude gesture behind Sisko's back, and now Worf complained bitterly that O'Brien had talked him into accepting the writer. But without prompting, Asta-ha at the bottom already put her fingers into her mouth and blew two short, sharp whistles, followed by a longer third.

Owena-da, supervising the drop from the top, sent another man, Rimtha-da, down the parallel rope. Rimtha-da was the largest of the Tiffnakis, and he slid perhaps a little too slowly but steadily down his own rope until he was next to Drukulu-da.

Rimtha-da hooked himself to the trapped man with one loose carabiner, then got Drukulu-da to put his weight on Rimtha-da while the latter unjammed the rope. Then both men untethered and slid down their respective ropes to a chorus of undulating whistles, which Chief O'Brien decided was the Whatsit version of applause.

Nobody lost his cool, and what was most astonishing, they cooperated on an *innovative solution* to a sudden problem. "My God," said O'Brien somewhat sarcastically to his Klingon friend, "there's an improvement already: they didn't even start checking the cliff face for new tech." Worf merely grunted in response; but it was his all-right-so-maybe-I-was-wrong-for-once-in-my-life grunt, and O'Brien understood.

When the Tiffnakis came to the bog, they had a slight setback. Someone found another force beam projector carelessly left on the ground, and Owena-da started to use it. But when Sisko strode up angrily, the weapons master shuffled his feet like Molly caught with her hand in Keiko's *mochi* jar, and he handed over the device.

"Target practice, Worf," shouted the captain, throwing the projector high in the air over the swamp. For the first time on this planet, the Klingon drew his service phaser and fired a short blast, all in one fluid motion. The device exploded noisily, making the point more brutally than any number of words could have: when the Natives ran up against the Cardassians, the invaders could make *all* the tech, new or old, vanish as quickly if not as dramatically as Worf had just "vanished" the force beam projector.

O'Brien was fascinated to see what *low*-tech method the Tiffnaki commandos would invent to get across the swamp; the final technique, masterminded by Owena-da and Asta-ha, but with input from virtually everyone in the platoon, was impressive enough that Chief Miles Edward O'Brien awarded it his *"Croix des Cerveaux"* with cukoonut clusters: the Tiffnakis retreated a kilometer to a forest they had bypassed; using knives they improvised out of the sharp pieces of shale that seemed to be everywhere on Sierra-Bravo 112-II, they hacked down a number of small saplings.

They spent two hours tying the saplings together and covering them with wide, palmlike fronds of some local fern; when they finished, they had a pair of long, flat "minibridges" with half a dozen stubby legs about a meter long on either side. Each minibridge was long enough that the entire platoon, including the away team "officers" (counting Odo, Quark, and O'Brien as officers for the sake of discussion), could stand along it without much crowding.

Then they returned to the bog. Placing the first minibridge down into the muck, Asta-ha led the way onto it. The plank sank into the mud, but nowhere near as deeply as an individual person would; the muddy water that slooshed across the top was easily waded.

Once the entire platoon was onto the minibridge, they passed the second across the tops of their heads to drop it into the muck in front of the first. Once everybody had traversed onto the second plank, the team—they were truly working as a team now—drew up the first by means of twisted-vine ropes. Passing it along overhead, they repeated the process all the way across the swamp, arriving in half the time it would have taken to wade, and with perhaps a tenth of the mud clinging to their legs and torsos as Quark had when he had played Diving for Latinum a few days earlier, on the first, abortive Scouting trip.

Even Captain Sisko admitted it was a brilliant improvisation . . . but he said he would reserve judgment until they returned to the main regiment of Tiffnakis. But Chief O'Brien was already starting to feel the swell of pride that he always got when "his" recruits began to shine.

Owena-da got the award for Conspicuous Obviousness when, after long minutes of silent thought on the part of all the commandos, he was the one to figure out how to ford the rushing river: they put their best rope thrower up in a tree with a vine rope, and he lassoed the opposite tree.

Alas, when they tried to shimmy from one to the other, the vine rope stretched enough that everyone got a thorough dunking in the angry river . . . as O'Brien had secretly suspected would happen. Fortunately, the chief insisted that everyone tether to the tightrope using the carabiners, so no one was washed away. Chief O'Brien sighed and took his dunking when his turn came. "Well, at least it's washed away the rest of that muck," he told Odo on the other bank. Odo was most annoyed at having to get wet. *Probably wishes he could've just turned back into a hawk and flown over,* thought O'Brien, smiling to himself.

The biggest obstacle faced by the commandos was the lake, which the captain added as an afterthought after seeing how well they did on the bog. Chief O'Brien paced to and from the shoreline, watching the Natives spread along the lakeshore, pointing to the other side and talking excitedly. Whenever they used the newly discovered "tech" of exerting their brains for innovation and problem-solving, they tended to yell at each other in excited tones and flutter their hands up and down directly in front of their chests . . . either a cultural or evolutionary characteristic, the chief wasn't sure.

The patrician but still good-looking Asta-ha, with her straight, bluish blond hair and small, boyish figure, wrapped her cloak around herself and said nothing, staring directly across the water with an unwavering gaze and mumbling to herself. Owena-da drew figures in the wet sand of various "weapon techs" he had seen or heard about, wondering if any of them would help them across. The other Tiffnakis offered exaggerated and increasingly fantastical suggestions, ineluctably reminding O'Brien of the scene in the holoplay *Cyrano de Bergerac*, where the seventeenth-century courtier-swordsman extemporizes twelve methods of flying from Earth to the moon (including a sedan chair drawn by geese and a hot-air balloon).

"Keiko made me go see that play," he muttered to himself . . . going insane trying to stop himself suggesting the obvious solution: a raft. "And I'm glad she did."

"I beg your pardon?" asked Odo, standing directly behind the chief. O'Brien jumped guiltily; he hadn't heard the constable come up behind him. *But then, no one ever does,* he consoled himself.

"Sorry, Odo; I was remembering a holoplay that Keiko made us attend. Actually, I wanted to go; but sometimes it's a good thing"—he leaned forward and gave the constable a wink—"to be reluctantly dragged away and then gush about how much you enjoyed it. Good for the marriage, I mean."

Odo shook his head in puzzlement. "I'm afraid I *still* can't understand why you play so many games with your relationships. Isn't it enough simply to enjoy common interests, without having to trick your wife into believing she convinced you against your will?"

O'Brien shrugged, so very paradoxical—*a pregnant Irish bull,* he half remembered from somewhere. "What could be more fun than playing silly games with the woman you love?" But thinking of Keiko made him long for her, and Molly. O'Brien grinned a somewhat goofy, cockeyed smile. "I really miss them, Odo. I miss them both; I miss the station. Damn it, *why* do we have to leave? Even if Kai Winn is in charge, all right, I can accept that; but why do we have to leave?"

"I hate to say it, but I miss the station whenever I'm away," said the constable, surprising O'Brien. "I'll . . . probably be asked to depart permanently as well. Somehow, I can't picture the Kai using any security officers but her own. And I must admit, there are several Bajoran deputies on my staff who would make reasonably adequate constables." The constable pulled a long face, literally. "I wonder whether I can accompany Captain Sisko to his next billet?"

"I wonder how they're doing," mused the chief. "I'll bet Keiko really has her hands full, trying to pack *and* take care of Molly." He sighed, thinking of *Deep Space Nine*, his home for the last four years, . . . the home he probably would never see again after returning and immediately departing.

O'Brien continued to pace and grumble to himself for another hour before the struggling Tiffnakis finally hit on the idea of a raft. They had a hard time with the concept of buoyancy at first; Asta-ha (an early raft convert) required every gram of persuasion at her command to convince the rest of the commandos that Dalvda-ha's "floating bridge" would actually float: "You know Tivva-ma, you know she is strong in the tech. My Tivva-ma has floated such toys herself on the Electromagnetic River southeast of the village. . . . Some of your own children have done so with Tivva-ma; and you, Owena-da, have even seen the sticks she floats."

"But those are sticks, Mayor Asta-ha. How can you compare a stick to a bridge? The bridge is far larger, hence it will sink. A great rock sinks faster than a tiny pebble, doesn't it?"

O'Brien listened, fascinated in an abstract sort of way. Knowing the answer so deeply—Archimedes' principle was still one of the first engineering concepts taught at school, even three thousand years after its discovery on Earth (and thirty thousand years after the Vulcans figured it out)—it was incredibly hard for the chief to put himself in the position of someone who literally had *never heard of a boat*. The principle was actually not as self-evident as it seemed from his perspective. *I mean,* he thought, *why SHOULD a big, heavy object float on top of the water?*

But finally, the girls, Asta-ha and Dalvda-ha, persuaded the rest of the commandos to give it a try. After a number of false starts, occupying the better part of a day, they put together a passable raft that passed inspection with the captain. It carried them across the lake and within five kilometers of the place along the tributary river where the rest of the Tiffnakis waited (they hoped). But by the time they arrived, it was well into night, and the greater moon had already set; Sisko decreed they would start out in the morning. "Tonight," said the captain, "when the troops have gone to sleep, I shall see the away team in my tent."

Two hours passed uneventfully. The Natives, after some instruction and training sessions, managed to get a fire started using a bowstring to rotate a stick in a hole. It was an ancient military technique, but Chief O'Brien hadn't learned it in Starfleet. . . . He'd picked it up watching old American Western holoplays. Oddly enough, it worked; other Tiffnakis were experimenting with a hastily woven gill net, and fish aplenty (with legs!) were caught for dinner. The away team ate more com-rats in silence; O'Brien found his nearly as inedible as Native food would be.

As O'Brien saw Worf stealing through the night toward the commanding officer's tent, and just before the chief himself was to leave, Odo sidled up. "I've just had the most disturbing conversation with that female," said Odo, looking stuffier than usual.

O'Brien shrugged. "Should've taken my advice; women like a little mystery."

"Oh, get your mind off such nonsense. That—that lady mayoress just came up to me and asked if I . . ." He looked sideways, left, right; O'Brien found himself doing the same, though he had no idea what he was looking for. "She asked me if I was going to *turn into jelly* again anytime soon."

"Well? Are you?"

"Yes, of course. But that's not the point, you—that's not the point, Chief O'Brien." Odo sucked in his lower lip and glared back at the Tiffnakis, who were beginning to snore (they made an irritating hissing noise, less like sawing logs than frying bacon). "The point is, Chief, that she saw me shapechange." He lowered his voice to a conspiratorial whisper. "Despite all my precautions. They must have excellent eyesight. But she and who else? Do they *all* know I'm a shapechanger?"

"Odo, I don't know what to say. I know the captain ordered you not to shapechange, but he knows you can't hold your form longer than sixteen hours."

As O'Brien led the way; Odo said nothing more about the incident . . . and the chief was amused to notice that the constable said nothing to Captain Sisko, either; evidently, Odo had been paying attention after all to O'Brien's oratory about the games solids play.

CHAPTER
16

THE ENTIRE AWAY TEAM was at the meeting, of course, and it was the first time O'Brien could remember in days that they had all gotten together *as a team,* without anyone but themselves in attendance. *Just us,* he thought; *just us alien invaders.* Sisko sat at the far end of his inflatable tent, the fire burned down to embers between him and the open door. The rest of the team filed in one at a time and found a seat. O'Brien sat cross-legged, closest to the tent flap, so he could keep an eye behind them, at the commandos huddled on the open ground, without tent or blanket: he still didn't quite trust this planet.

"We are in danger of allowing this mission to run away with us," said the captain gravely, his thoughts seeming to echo the chief's. "We've allowed ourselves—*I* have allowed us—to integrate more thoroughly into this planet's culture than I intended. From now on, I mean to be the captain of the *Defiant* away team . . . not the general of the Sierra-Bravo defense force."

O'Brien spoke up. "It was a good plan, sir, if I do say so. But it's done; we've set them on the road. . . . Isn't this their fight from now on?"

"You are missing the point," objected Worf. "We are not helping one side in an internal power struggle. The *Cardassians,* not we, have interfered in the planet's development."

"Worf is right," Sisko adjudicated. "This is still our fight, Chief, but I don't want us leading the Native charge, if you can see the distinction."

"Perhaps," said Odo, "we should confront the Cardassians personally, ourselves, not surrounded by a mob of native life-forms."

"But how?" demanded the chief. It was a great speech on the captain's part, but vague on the details. "How are we five to stop the Cardassians and a thousand Drek'la foot soldiers, or even slow them down? Perhaps the best we can do is stay here and lead the troops into battle."

"No, Chief; that's too close an involvement. We should face them directly. . . . Somehow." O'Brien swallowed, and neither Quark nor Odo looked particularly happy.

Worf, however, showed a terrible, frightening

Klingon grin of battle joy. "Yes. . . . Perhaps tomorrow will be a good day to die."

Here we go again, thought Chief O'Brien, but the captain was surprisingly on Worf's side. "Yes, Commander, perhaps it will. But in the meanwhile, I'd rather stay alive a while longer and burn the Cardassians rather more than we have so far."

Quark, who had remained silent throughout the exchange, could no longer contain himself. He burst forth with a cynical yet truthful observation: *"More* than we have? We haven't burned them at all." Snarling and muttering darkly, the little Ferengi paced up and down. "I can see where this is going. . . . Nowhere. None of you has a clue how to handle the situation."

"Oh," jeered Odo, "and I suppose you do?"

Quark sighed, shaking his head as if speaking to a six-year-old; O'Brien fought the impulse to wind up and kick the barkeeper into the next campfire. "Of course I, personally, would have plenty of better ideas, because I, personally, have a code of life to live by."

"Oh, of *course.* The Federation Code of Criminal Offenses. How shortsighted of me."

"I'm talking about the Rules of Acquisition, you runny-faced bucket-sitter." O'Brien noticed that when Quark got really piqued, his face turned almost bright pink, the color of the flowers of the deep Glen Tsismusk on Bajor.

Sisko interrupted smoothly, trying to keep the argument on some productive track. "Do you have a particular Rule of Acquisition in mind, Mr. Quark?"

The Ferengi paused, taking a long glare at Odo before saying, "Yes, Captain; as a matter of fact, one has been lodged in my planet-sized brain ever since we saw the Cardassian attack on Brew—on Druvis-miss-niss-whatever the heck it is."

Quark paused as if finished.

"Well?" demanded O'Brien; Worf glowered and Odo snorted; only Captain Sisko seemed to have enough patience to outwait the melodramatic Ferengi.

"I've been almost obsessed with the two hundred and eighty-fourth Rule," said Quark.

Sisko spoke up instantly: "Deep down, *everyone's* a Ferengi."

Quark's eyes widened. "Very good, Captain! Better than Rom, as I'm sure you're not surprised to hear."

Odo snorted again, even more loudly. "Typical Ferengi arrogance. All right, Quark, *how* is everyone deep down a Ferengi, and how does that help us?"

"It means that when you push anyone hard enough, he'll manage to find a core of ingenuity somewhere within him. . . . Though I admit, the rule does seem to have one or two exceptions—Odo."

"All right; so how do we push them hard enough?" prompted the captain.

"My next thought was of Rule Forty-Four. . . . Do you know that one, Captain?"

Sisko smiled. "I memorized them all; it's not that difficult, and good mental discipline. Never confuse wisdom with luck."

O'Brien was starting to catch the Ferengi's drift. "The Cardassians, right? They've won every battle, and they probably think it's because of their brilliant tactics. But it's really just their luck that they landed *here,* where the power-cutting trick works such magic."

"You see, Odo? If only the hu-mans would start to teach the Rules of Acquisition in Starfleet Academy, they could rule the . . . wait. Forget I said anything."

"All right. So the Cardassians have been winning because of their luck, that the Natives never learned how to respond to the loss of all their toys; but if you scratch them hard enough, like we've seen here, all that inborn ingenuity comes back, and suddenly they're a formidable enemy. So what's the key, Quark? What's the magic bullet to connect Forty-Four with Two Hundred and Eighty-Four?"

Quark smiled, then curled his lip in a snarl of triumph in Odo's direction. "The Rule that keeps me alive on *Deep Space Nine,* or *Terek Nor,* or whatever it ends up being called tomorrow: It's always good business to know about new customers *before* they walk in your door."

"One Hundred and Ninety-Four," muttered Sisko.

"Or in this case," concluded the Ferengi, "it's good strategy to know all about a new Cardassian tactic before they use it on *you.*"

Sisko stared at Quark. In the wink of an eye, the mad scheme had become crystal clear. "Quark . . . you're suggesting we cut the power *over the entire planet* at once."

"Cut the power on the whole planet?" asked Worf, not following the logic.

"Worf, it's brilliant!" Chief O'Brien felt more alive, excited than he had since transporting down to the forsaken, senseless planet. "What's the one big advantage the invaders have in every battle?"

"They cut the power broadcast and render the Native weapons useless. But I do not see how this—"

"But it's not that the toys stop working, Worf; it's that they stop working just before the fight. And the Natives are so shaken by the sudden loss of everything that they can't even mount a defense at the level of spears and swords."

"Slings," said the captain, "arrows, traps—everything that a poorly armed and equipped band of freedom fighters ever used to bring a superpower to a grinding halt."

"So we cut the power *first*"—O'Brien was in his element, explaining something—"and by the time the Cardassians get to the next village, the Natives'll have already had days or even weeks to get used to the new way of things."

Sisko nodded. "I must admit, Quark, it's a plan."

"It's a ridiculous plan," objected Odo, "and it's totally illegal. We can't go around cutting the power of people who depend upon technology for their very survival. How are they to eat? How will they defend themselves against each other?"

Sisko grinned. "Constable, you have hit the nail square on the head. That's it exactly: they *will* find a way to eat, to defend themselves against other Natives—and to defend themselves against the Cardassians."

Chief O'Brien blinked. *Well, Constable, there's yet another example for you.* The chief chuckled. "Beats me why they don't just accept reality and repeal the bloody thing," he said. Nobody paid attention.

The captain rose, his head just brushing the ceiling of the tent. "Gentlemen, we have our plan: we will find the central power generators for the whole planet and kick them off-line. . . . Temporarily, at least. Chief, put together an action plan for finding them, and work with Worf to profile what sort of generators the planet would need and how we might sabotage them. Odo . . . be prepared to infiltrate the Cardassian camp; we must find out whether the chief was right, and they're fugitives from the empire—or whether this truly is a front in a new war. . . . And whether there is a Founder among them."

Chief Miles Edward O'Brien rose first, followed by the rest. *Full plate,* he thought, happy for the first time since arriving in orbit and looking over Dax's shoulder at the technology readout; at last, there was something positive to *do.*

But how humiliating that it was Quark who had to think of the key. The only point that made the embarrassment bearable was when O'Brien thought of poor Odo . . . stuck with a Ferengi who would never forget or allow the constable to do so. . . . For years and years, if the chief were a good judge of character.

That is, assuming they all lived that long.

Major Kira Nerys stood in the Kai's private audience chamber, what once had been Captain Sisko's office, overlooking Ops and the fatigued, frustrated, but still utterly professional defense team. The station shuddered regularly now with the pounding from alien invaders attached to the hull, as they tried to bore their way by hand through the containment field and the station's outer skin. The enemy worked its way at every joint and join, and *still* Kira had no idea in the world who the bloody attackers were!

She paced back and forth, parallel to Kai Winn's desk, mumbling inaudibly to herself. The Kai seemed perfectly calm, adding to Kira's fury; "serene" is the word that popped into the major's head: *That blasted woman is always so damned SERENE. I can't take any more of it.*

Kira turned her back on the Kai, so the woman wouldn't see the tears of a chained attack dog. "I should be out there. People are dying!"

"Your place is here, child."

"I should be fighting! I'm a warrior—I fought in the underground, I should be fighting now to defend this—this little piece of Bajor from the Prophets know what is trying to worm under our skin." Kira whirled to face Kai Winn. "Can't you understand that?"

Stunned, Kira stared again at the sensors, the viewers; both showed the same tragic scene: four Bajoran cruisers sliced open like dissected animals, their guts streaming into space. The invaders hadn't even bothered either to rescue or to kill the survivors of the ill-fated effort to relieve the station. There might be another expedition, but not soon. The rest of the Bajoran navy was desperately needed to defend the planet . . . assuming the pirates from the Gamma Quadrant next turned their attention thither. There was no help from the homeworld, no help from home.

The Kai shook her head. "You are the one who does not understand, child," she said sadly. "The senior officer's place is not at the head of the troops, where he could be slain by a single lucky shot. His place is behind the lines, at the nerve center, where he can control his followers."

Kira shook her head, astonished. "You talk as if

you know *what you're talking about,*" she said; the words began in respect but ended in a scream of fury. "What do you know about fighting?"

It was an unfair charge; the Kai had done remarkably well so far. The enemy (whoever they were) had not yet penetrated the station itself; they had managed to slither inside the defensive screen of *DS9*—rather, the *Emissary's Sanctuary;* but there, they had so far stalemated: they crawled all along the skin of the station in bulky black pressure suits, hacking and chopping and trying to drill their way inside. But in another sense, it was something Kira had to clear from her conscience. "Kai Winn, with the deepest, most profound respect, I must say that I know a lot more about this sort of fighting than you . . . and I should be there in the thick, leading the troops—Bajoran troops—to victory."

Behind the words, inside her head, Major Kira came to a decision at that very moment that made the tragedy complete: orders or no, Kira Nerys decided that she had no choice but to broadcast a Priority One distress call to the nearest Federation ship, begging for assistance from Starfleet. It meant the end of her dream of a Bajoran *Deep Space Nine,* but not to do so would strike the final gong for the station and everyone inside, and perhaps for Bajor itself. *I have no choice!* she screamed silently.

She would do it the next time she was able to leave Ops, which if the Kai had her way, would be never. But Kira would find a way to deliver the message; she always did.

In the meanwhile, Kira stood rigidly opposite her Kai, the people's Kai, the freely elected (in a sense) leader of the government of Bajor—the self-selected governor of *Emissary's Sanctuary*. Kira had to talk about something, make conversation; there was nothing else to do for the moment. The alien attackers controlled everything from the skin of the station outward; the Bajorans owned the flesh, blood, heart, and brains beneath. Unless there was a breakthrough—*Prophets forbid!*—Kira was a helpless, caged animal, useful only to wait, and wait, for penetration.

But the Kai was taking this all calmly, as if she'd been through it all before. "Kai Winn," Kira asked, "I know a Bajoran doesn't ask another this question, and if you don't want to answer, I'll understand."

"Why child, what could I possibly want to conceal?"

Yeah, right. "Kai . . . what *did* you do during the Occupation?" The reason it was considered terribly impolite to ask such a thing was the huge numbers of Bajorans who were forced by necessity and empty stomachs to cooperate with the puppet government established and run by Gul Dukat, who ruled from his iron fist in orbit, from the dreaded *Terek Nor*. Why drag through the mud the last shreds of dignity an old, frightened woman might still possess? Even if she was the Kai.

"During the Occupation?" The Kai seemed quite genuinely suprised. "I'd . . . just as soon not discuss it."

Stunned by the sudden turn of events—the Kai had actually accepted the challenge—Kira relaxed slowly into a chair, staring at the seemingly stubborn, old woman. Kai Winn began to speak, her voice so soft, it caressed Kira's cheek like the wind through the trees of Glen Tsismusk.

"But if you have to know . . . the Occupation began before I was born, but by the time I turned twenty-one, before you were born, child, I was the primary house slave to a young Cardassian gul—a gentle man, as far as that went." The Kai smiled disarmingly, winking at Kira. "But that's not *all* I was, my child; you freedom fighters were not the only enemies of Cardassia."

Kira waited, breathlessly . . . but that was all the answer she got.

The (fake) walls of the (ersatz) runabout cracked under the (pretended) pressure of the hulking sea. Jadzia Dax licked dry lips inside her scuba helmet—the holo-simulation was so real, too real!—and spoke through a (faintly) cracking larynx over the comm link. "How . . . how much pressure, Julian?"

Bashir looked at the gauge as the runabout lurched in the current. "I read it as seventy-three standard atmospheres."

"No, I don't mean in the simulation. I mean for

real. How much pressure as soon as we exit the *Defiant?*"

The puzzled doctor stared sideways at Dax, turning his whole body, since his head and neck were constrained by his own helmet. "Jadzia, you know the answer to that better than I. The ship currently sits at approximately one hundred and seventy atmospheres."

"Enough," she said, almost to herself, "enough to crush a runabout like a . . ."

"An egg?"

She smiled wanly. "We already used that one. Crush us like some . . . small, crushable thing."

Bashir reached across, piercing her with his limpid, brown eyes, seen through the faceplate, putting a heavily gloved hand on her arm. "Steady, Commander. We'll be all right. It was your own calculations." He gestured with his head at the seawater beyond the (holo) hull of the (holo) runabout. "It appears to be working, you see? Your calculations are correct. Shields down to forty percent. We should rupture and lose pressurization in about six minutes."

"Computer," said Dax quietly, "end program."

The two of them stood, still absurdly attired in deep-ocean scuba gear. Dax cracked her seals and removed her helmet, just in time to be berated by her aqua-comrade.

"Jadzia, *why* did you do that?" Bashir stared in open-mouthed irritation.

She shook her head. "It's no good, Julian. It's not the real thing . . . but it's too real. If I do this now, I might not be able to do it for real, when the time comes."

The doctor pressed his lips together, stared at the walls, floor, and ceiling of criss-crossing lines of holoemitters. "You don't want to rehearse?"

"Not my death, Julian."

Bashir sighed. "It was the one thing keeping me from screaming in terror." He snorted. "All right, we'll split the difference. We've already practiced the first ninety meters; I suppose we'll just wing it the rest of the way."

Shrugging in apology, Jadzia turned and left the holodeck, leaving Dr. Bashir behind. Pride held her rigid through the passageway, down the turbo-lift, and into her quarters.

Only then did she allow herself to collapse on the bed, shaking like an out-of-balance turbine. She fell into a thrashing, fitful sleep and dreamt of trillions of tons of poisoned water crushing host and symbiote alike into undifferentiated constituent atoms.

"But what *did* you do during the Occupation, Kai?" persisted Major Kira.

"I kept myself occupied, child." Kai Winn fidgeted; she was determined not to fall into the sin of living in the past, as did so many others who suffered through the decades of brutal occupation. It was such a common failing! So many people, decent people who loved the Prophets and tried to live as kind and good a life as possible, too many began nearly every sentence with a sigh, a glance flickered over the shoulder—as if there might be a Cardassian informer in the next booth—and words like, "Back during the Troubles, I—" or "It's not like it was during the Bad Times, when I . . ."

I will NOT be one of those people, Kai Winn firmly told herself. She despised such people. *No, that's not fair; I despise that evasion, but I pity such people.* Pity was a very unpopular emotion, but it was one of the most decent (when it wasn't used as a euphemism for "look down upon").

"I resisted, child." Finally, the Kai's young protégée—surely Kira didn't know she was a protégée!—took the hint and sat down, still trembling like a racing beast waiting for the gong. The Kai felt a terrible sympathy; Kai Winn had been through so much, so much more than anyone realized, that this small attack could not pierce her shield. She knew she was not fated to die at the hands of unknown aliens in the Emissary's own sanctuary; she had looked into the Orb and seen herself older, seen struggles ahead. She didn't know just when she would die (thank the Prophets!), but she knew it was not now, not here.

There is a great comfort in *knowing* one will survive one's present difficulties; Kira had no such certainty, the poor dear. *Just as I had no certainty*

*during the Occupation that Nerys so obsesses upon;
I knew not what Gul Ragat would take it into his
head to do next.*

Stop! The Kai wrenched her mind out of the
indulgent groove and returned to the present time.
She could see that the past could not be suppressed
utterly; it would out now and again. But she would
control it, at least awaiting a more opportune
moment. Perhaps during the night; Kira, who just
arrived on duty after a fitful five hours of supposed
rest, would take command while Kai Winn returned to her own quarters in the back of what had
been the Emissary's ready room.

*Then will be the time; then I will allow the
demons of the past to engulf me . . . for a little
while.*

In the meanwhile, she had to manage the battle.
"Child, there has been no new assault while you
slept. The Gamma Quadrant aliens are maintaining their siege positions, but I'm sure they're planning something."

"I don't think they're just going to give up, my
Kai. They've invested too much—and they've
killed people on the Bajoran destroyers. They must
know we won't let them simply leave!" Kira's skin
darkened as the blood rushed to her face. She was
desperately suppressing an emotion that could
overwhelm her senses if she allowed it.

Don't slip the floodgates, warned the Kai silently.
"They know," agreed Winn. "They're planning to

breech the station manually. They've been scanning us continually, very high-level scans."

"Looking for a crack?"

Kai Winn nodded.

"Is there a crack, my Kai?"

The Kai shrugged. "Probably. It's in the hands of the Prophets; we can only do what we can do, imperfect beings that we are."

Nerys seemed glumly dissatisfied with this response as well. She stood and slid down the ladderway to the main level of Operations; there she paced around the central control panels, probably distracting the Kai's personal defense squad, who manned the battle stations.

Kai Winn sighed, wishing she could as easily give vent to her anxieties as her young protégée. But the Prophets were strict: they required self-control and discipline. The Kai smiled, imagining what Major Kira of the Shakaar resistance cell would think if Kai Winn were to tell her the destiny she envisioned for Nerys: that someday, and not too far into the future, Nerys would herself hear the call of the Prophets, . . . and would take holy orders, eventually succeeding Winn as Kai.

She'd probably laugh in my face, then turn bright red with horror! Kai Winn smiled at the thought. She hoped someday to see confirmation of her vision in the Orb; until then, it was a mere possibility, nothing more.

Nerys, thought the Kai, *forgive me, but you would*

make an excellent priestess; if only you could believe it!

The last hour of the Kai's shift passed uneventfully. When she felt the fatigue of her aging body overtake her brain, she knew it was time to hand over the reins. "Nerys," she said, catching the young officer's attention; Kira looked up, surprised at the familiarity of her given name. "Take command. I must rest; remember my authority, Major. . . . Do nothing to undermine it."

Kira's face burned red again, and she couldn't look the Kai in the face. "I—I will, my Kai. I mean I won't." Kai Winn smiled as she turned away to the ready room. *She's going to betray me, she thinks; she's going to call the Federation for help against the invaders.* But of course, it was all part of the Prophets' plan . . . whatever Kira chose to do.

Yawning fiercely, Kai Winn took stately, measured steps into her new office, overlooking Ops, and ordered the door shut. Then she relaxed and became an older woman once more. A few hours of just being Winn—not Kai nor vedek nor interpreter of the Prophets—was what she urgently needed.

Just being Winn, like the young girl who found herself, a newly minted sister, assigned to tend the spiritual needs of Gul Ragat's Bajoran slaves . . . and a slave herself, of course. Sister Winn was not a warrior. *What did you do in the Resistance? I may not have carried a gun and planted bombs, but child, I surely resisted!* And how much harder it always was to resist *without* weapons. . . . Something the soldiers never seemed to appreciate.

Remaining appropriately dressed, in case she was summoned from sleep by an emergency, Kai Winn lay carefully on the bed that once was the Emissary's emergency cot, feeling a small, girlish thrill at being so close to the man so personally blessed by the Prophets—who *spoke* to them directly! She barely closed her eyes, giving herself final permission to let the dead past rise, when she found herself dreaming of days gone by. . . . She was back in Governor Legate Migar's mansion attending the young and dashing Gul Ragat, subgovernor of the Bajoran provinces of Shakarri and Belshakarri. . . .

TO BE CONTINUED IN
Star Trek: Deep Space Nine
Rebels
Book Two
The Courageous

Look for STAR TREK Fiction from Pocket Books

Star Trek®: The Original Series

Star Trek: The Next Generation®

Star Trek: Deep Space Nine®

Star Trek®: Voyager™

Flashback • Diane Carey
The Black Shore • Greg Cox
Mosaic • Jeri Taylor

Star Trek®: New Frontier

Star Trek®: Day of Honor

Star Trek®: The Captain's Table

Book One: *War Dragons* • L. A. Graf
Book Two: *Dujonian's Hoard* • Michael Jan Friedman
Book Three: *The Mist* • Dean W. Smith & Kristine K. Rusch
Book Four: *Fire Ship* • Diane Carey
Book Five: *Once Burned* • Peter David
Book Six: *Where Sea Meets Sky* • Jerry Oltion

Star Trek®: The Dominion War

Book 1: *Behind Enemy Lines* • John Vornholt
Book 2: *Call to Arms . . .* • Diane Carey
Book 3: *Tunnel Through the Stars* • John Vornholt
Book 4: *. . . Sacrifice of Angels* • Diane Carey